Life's funny, sometimes. You think you've got your life mapped out the way you want it. Then, wham! Everything goes haywire.

I should have known that Dani Devereaux would cause me all kinds of grief. Hadn't I grown up living next door to her? Of course, I'd do whatever I could for her, please understand that, but marriage seemed a little drastic to me.

Then again, maybe it was just what I needed to really open my eyes and take a good look at her. Somehow, she managed to grow up without my noticing.

I guess there are worse things in the world than marrying a woman you think you know so well...especially when you discover you don't really know her at all!

Nick Montgomery

Please address questions and book requests to: Silhouette Reader Service
U.S.: 3010 Walden Ave., P.O. Box 1325, Buffalo, NY 14269
Canadian: P.O. Box 609, Fort Erie, Ont. L2A 5X3

Make-Believe Matrimony

ANNETTE BROADRICK
MARRIED?!

Silhouette Books

Published by Silhouette Books
America's Publisher of Contemporary Romance

SILHOUETTE BOOKS
300 East 42nd St.,
New York, N.Y. 10017

ISBN 0-373-30127-8

MARRIED?!

This edition published by arrangement with Harlequin Books S.A.

® and TM are trademarks of Harlequin Books S.A., used under license.
Trademarks indicated with ® are registered in the United States Patent and
Trademark Office, the Canadian Trade Marks Office and in other countries.

Printed in U.S.A.

A Letter from the Author

Dear Reader,

I had a lot of fun with this story. The characters arrived in my head full-blown and immediately took over, each telling me their version of what happened. Sometimes it happens that way, which makes my job a little easier.

I also enjoy writing stories about friends who discover that their feelings for each other go deeper than they realized. Nothing appeals to me more than the thought of being married to my very best friend.

Annette Broadrick

Chapter One

Nick Montgomery poured sparkling wine into two crystal glasses sitting on the bar in front of him. He smiled to himself, anticipating what would happen next.

Seated on his elegant sofa and waiting for him to rejoin her was the woman he had carefully stalked for over a year now: Letitia Link, one of the bright new stars of Hollywood.

He'd been introduced to Letitia the year before when he'd been in L.A. negotiating his contract to write the screenplay for *Triumph for Two*, his first Broadway hit. He'd ended up making several trips between his home in Connecticut and the West Coast before signing.

Each time he'd been in California he'd managed to see Letitia. On one occasion they had lunch; another time dinner. He'd carefully planned his strategy until he could get her to visit him in the East.

When his newest play opened on Broadway he found the perfect reason to have her there: he'd asked her to accompany him to the opening night and the party planned for later.

She had agreed. She had flown to New York.

And now, after three days, when the success of the new play was assured by the rave reviews, she had agreed to come to his home for the weekend.

Nick had to remind himself that all of this was real. After all those years of writing, of countless rejections, he was now sought-after, his every utterance eagerly repeated, his every date speculated about in the gossip columns.

The celebrity status he could have done without, but the recognition of his writing efforts was a balm to his soul.

He turned and carried the glasses to where Letitia sat. He fought not to betray his reaction to her. God, but she was gorgeous, her flaming red hair cascading around her face and shoulders like a fiery halo, her seductive green eyes smiling up at him.

He sank down onto the sofa beside her and handed her one of the glasses.

"Thank you, Nicky," she said in her husky voice.

He smiled.

"I want you to know how pleased I am that you invited me up here. You've gained such a reputation for being a recluse that I feel honored you were willing to share your quiet retreat with me."

Nick took a sip of wine before he replied. "I appreciate the fact that you understand how I feel."

"Oh, I do, Nicky. Believe me, I do. Sometimes it seems as though our lives are no longer our own."

He watched her take a sip of the wine, then touch her moist bottom lip with her tongue, as though to savor the flavor.

She glanced around the room. "Have you lived here long?"

"Three years."

"It's lovely, truly it is. Have you always lived in Connecticut?"

"No. I was born in New Jersey and lived there in a town called Teaneck until I left for college. As a matter of fact, my mother still lives there."

"So you're within visiting distance."

His mind flashed back to his old neighborhood and several childhood memories. Why was it whenever he thought of his past Dani always popped into his mind? Why wouldn't she stay in the past where she belonged?

Danielle Devereaux. Her name had always sounded more impressive than she looked. She'd been the bane of his childhood existence. Five years younger than he was, Dani had followed him around like a friendly puppy, wanting to play.

Their parents had been the greatest of friends, which had made living next door to each other a boon, but there had been times when Nick had wished to increase the difference between the two of them by several states.

Not that Dani had always been a pest, of course. It only seemed that way in retrospect. It was just that she was always underfoot, and the age difference when they were growing up had been too much to allow a companion-type relationship to form.

Let's face it, he thought, she'd had a constant crush on him that had never failed to embarrass him. All of his friends had teased him about it. Whenever he blew up at her she would go home crying, making him feel like a complete heel, so that he would end up apologizing. Then she would continue following him around again.

Dani was a part of his past, a distant part at that. In fact he hadn't seen her in a couple of years. She had attended the opening night of his first show, he remembered.

Come to think of it, his female lead character had been based, very loosely of course, on Dani.

The audience had loved her—her zany sense of humor, her inability to stay out of trouble, her warmth and compassion.

Nick suddenly realized what he was doing. After all of his scheming, here he was finally with Letitia Link, and he was allowing his thoughts to wander to his childhood nemesis, Dani Devereaux.

Dear God. He must be losing his mind.

He reached over and gently lifted the glass from Letitia's graceful fingers. She smiled when she saw that he had put both glasses on the low table in front of them. He found encouragement in that smile, encouragement that he needed. His heart raced. He leaned toward her and with practiced ease drew her into his arms.

She lifted her face to his and in that moment Nick knew that his every desire was about to be fulfilled.

The doorbell rang.

His mouth had just settled on the luscious provocative lips that had teased and tantalized him for months when he heard the jangling interruption. He decided to ignore the sound.

The doorbell rang again with several short bursts of impatience and one long shrill sound that promised to continue through the night like an air-raid siren.

Nick groaned and reluctantly released the pliant woman in his arms.

"It sounds urgent," she whispered in the husky voice that caused chills to chase up and down his body.

"I'll have to get it. I gave the housekeeper the weekend off." He rose reluctantly and looked down at her. She smiled. "I'll get rid of whoever it is and be right back."

"I promise to be here waiting."

He grinned, then headed for the door. Whoever it was had better have a damned good reason for interrupting him. He strode into the hall muttering unprintable imprecations at the idiot who continued to lean on his door bell.

Nick jerked the door open. "What do you—"

A tiny young female stood on his doorstep, staring up at him with imploring black eyes. Tousled black curls clung to her ears and framed her face. She wore a baggy sweatshirt with a suggestive logo emblazoned on its front and snug jeans that were torn at the knees and on one thigh.

As soon as she saw him her pale frightened expression changed into one of hope, as though she had at last discovered the savior she'd been seeking. In truth, she had.

Before he could say anything she threw herself at him, her arms wrapped around his waist, her head buried in his chest.

"Oh, thank God you're home, Nick. I had almost given up. I didn't know what I was going to do. The police are looking for me and I couldn't think. You've got to help me!"

Nick still had the doorknob in his hand and was staring at the now empty doorstep, feeling as though he'd been run over by a truck.

"Dani! What in the hell is going on! What are you doing here? And why are the police after you?" He glanced outside once again, then closed the door.

"You've got to help me, Nick. I don't know what to do."

He sighed. "Dani, would you let go of me? I can't understand what you're mumbling into my shirt."

Slowly she let go of the death grip she had around his waist and looked up at him. "Please don't be angry with me, Nick. I honestly didn't know where else to turn. When the security guard yelled at me I lost my nerve and ran. I managed to get away from the plant but then the police started following me. I couldn't stop and explain. I knew that they wouldn't believe me. I was afraid to go home. Then I remembered that you lived several miles north of the plant so I—"

"Whoa, whoa, wait a minute. I can't make head nor tails out of what you're saying. Besides that, I have company. Why don't you come back on Monday and I'll see what I can—"

"Monday! But this is only Friday. And I don't dare go home. What if the police got my license number? They'll be waiting for me—"

"Damn it, Dani! What do you want from me?"

She dropped her eyes to the scuffed toes of her faded sneakers. "I was hoping you'd let me hide here for the weekend. No one would ever guess that I'd come here. By Monday maybe I can figure out whether I should try to return to work, as though nothing happened, or—"

"You are not staying here and that's final."

Dani seemed to wilt in front of him. He didn't know how she managed to do that. She looked as though she were shrinking into herself. God, he hated it when she did that. Furious with her for making him feel guilty, he attacked. "Why are you dressed like that? You look all of twelve years old."

Which was true. In the baggy sweatshirt, without makeup and with her short curly hair tousled, her wide black eyes staring up at him, she could have passed for a child. Why couldn't Dani have grown up like the rest of the kids on the block? She had barely managed to reach five feet when she stopped growing.

"Is this young lady a friend of yours, Nicky?"

Nick froze for an instant before turning to look at Letitia. She stood under the arch that formed the doorway between the foyer and his den looking delectable and seductive. He glanced at Dani and almost groaned. He recognized that expression on her face. Because of her lack of stature, Dani had at times gone along with the mistaken impression that she was a lot younger than her actual age. Now she stared at Letitia with large rounded eyes, her gaze reflecting the awe of a child seeing in person someone she recognized from the screen.

Slowly she turned her gaze toward Nick. "I had no idea you knew Letitia Link," she breathed in an innocent childlike voice that made Nick want to swat her on her backside. He knew very well how unimpressed Dani was with show business and the people involved. He watched as she took a couple of steps toward Letitia. "You're even more beautiful in person," she said in a hushed tone.

Letitia's smile embraced both Nick and Dani. "Why, thank you, my dear. That's very kind of you." Her gaze met Nick's. "Aren't you going to introduce me to your little friend?"

"This is Danielle Devereaux," Nick said through gritted teeth. "Our families are close friends."

Letitia extended her hand. "I'm very pleased to meet you, Danielle. Any friend of Nicky's is a friend of mine."

Nick tried not to flinch at the cliché.

Dani accepted the hand bestowed on her with suitable humility.

"Would you like to join us?" Letitia asked graciously.

"No!" Nick said firmly. When both women looked at him in obvious surprise he added hastily, "I, uh, that is, she just stopped by to, uh—"

"My mother had hoped Nick would let me sleep over since she had to go out of town unexpectedly."

Since Nick knew that Dani had not lived at home in the past seven years he was understandably incensed at her blatant lie.

"Dani . . ."

Letitia chuckled. "Do you get stuck with baby-sitting chores very often?"

"I'm afraid that Dani's not—"

"I promise not to cause you any trouble, Nick. Really I won't. I'll just go upstairs right now and go to bed. You won't even know I'm around."

Oh, yes I will!

"Nicky, you mustn't look so ferocious," Letitia teased. "You'll give her the impression she isn't wanted." She glanced at her watch. "I really need to be going, anyway. I had no idea of the time."

"But—"

"Why don't you call me a cab, Nicky? I'd love to stay and visit, but I think you're going to have your hands full for the weekend."

"Letitia, you don't understand. Dani is—"

Dani interrupted whatever he had been about to reveal about her by the simple act of throwing herself into his arms and bursting into tears.

Whatever he might do or say at this point would convince Letitia that he was an unfeeling monster. He looked at the redhead helplessly. "Where are you going to go?"

She shrugged. "Into town. I'm sure I'll find someplace to stay. Or I might rent a car and drive back to New York. I'll just play it by ear."

He stepped over to the hall phone with Dani still sobbing into his chest, made his call, then hung up the phone considering the possibilities of justifiable homicide.

God! He could wring Dani's neck!

"Go on upstairs," he muttered. She pulled away from him and he discovered that the tears hadn't been faked; the front of his shirt was soaked. He'd also noticed that she was shaking. She really was upset, no matter what else she had managed to do.

Dani turned away and started up the stairs.

"It was nice meeting you, Dani," Letitia said. "Perhaps I'll see you again."

Without looking up, Dani nodded. "G'night."

Dani had been at Nick's home only once before. She had been so scared it was nothing short of a miracle that she had found it tonight, she thought as she got to the top of the stairs.

Then she had seen Letitia and realized what she had done. Nick would never forgive her. Not ever. She swallowed a sob. Letitia Link was the embodiment of Nick's ideal woman. He had always been attracted to tall slender redheads, as far back as she could remember. Dani could have guessed that if given the opportunity he would certainly have pursued Letitia.

And now she had ruined his evening for him. As she peeked into each of the upstairs bedrooms, trying to decide where she should stay, she vowed to make it up to him somehow. She didn't mean to interfere with his love life. But it did seem as though she generally managed to mess up things for him.

Like the time when he'd been fifteen and had had a crush on one of the cheerleaders in junior high. He'd finally managed to get up enough nerve to ask her out... What was her name, anyway? Jody, that was it. He'd asked Jody to the dance after the basketball game. That was the time Dani had fallen in the bleachers and hurt her leg. The school officials had called her home but there had been no answer, so Nick had ended up seeing that she got home all right. He'd missed most of the dance and by the time he returned, as he took great pains to explain to Dani later, Jody had found someone else to dance with and had never accepted another date with him.

Dani groaned. She knew that she was the bane of Nick's existence. She didn't mean to be. Not really. She loved Nick. He was the brother she'd never had. Nick was the one she always turned to whenever things went wrong in her life.

And boy, had they suddenly gone wrong tonight.

She returned to the first bedroom at the top of the stairs and went inside. Obviously this was one of his guest bedrooms. She heard Nick in the hallway. When she peeked through the door she saw that he was carrying a small suitcase. Letitia had been planning to stay.

Now she *knew* Nick would never forgive her.

She sat on the edge of a chair and wearily untied her sneakers. Now that she was safe, the adrenaline she'd been running on had deserted her and she felt like a doll whose stuffing had all run out.

Dani pulled her sweatshirt over her head, baring her chest. She rarely wore a bra for the simple reason she didn't need one. Other small women had been blessed with adequate upper curves, but not her. At twenty-five she seldom gave her size or lack of size much thought, until she came face to face with a woman like Letitia Link, who appeared to have been given everything: looks, height and abundant curves.

After unzipping her jeans she stepped out of them and padded barefoot into the adjoining bathroom in her bikini briefs.

She glared at herself in the multimirrored room. Even undressed, she looked like an adolescent just beginning to bloom. Granted she had a tiny waist and rounded hips, and her legs were shapely and in proportion with the rest of her body. But she certainly wouldn't stop traffic.

Dani stood under the shower for a long time, hoping to wash away the weariness and the effects of the fright that had until a few minutes ago consumed her. Nick was going to demand an explanation. Actually he deserved one.

Looking back over the past few days Dani could see where she might have made one or two tiny errors in judgment. Hindsight was always so clear. She just hadn't realized in time what she had stumbled onto. By the time she *had* realized it, it was too late to back away and just report it to the authorities.

Somehow she knew that Nick would not understand her reasoning. He never did. He was always so good at lecturing her for her impulsiveness, as though he never made mistakes.

Like the time he'd gotten engaged to Katherine. Dani had tried to tell him what she was really like when no man was around, but he wouldn't listen. He'd been dazzled by her. If Dani hadn't managed to make her so angry that she'd lost her temper in front of Nick, he might have ended up married to a shrew without being aware of what he had chosen.

Of course he hadn't thanked Dani for saving him from such a fate. He never did understand that she had done it for his own good.

This time, however, her intentions had been pure. In fact, she hadn't been thinking of Nick at all. She had just naturally turned to him when she became aware that she was in way over her head.

She'd needed help. Nick was the one she had immediately sought.

Eventually Dani finished with her shower and got out of the tub. After towel drying her hair she found a comb and quickly ran it through her curls, leaving them to dry naturally. Then she wrapped the towel securely around her and returned to the bedroom.

Nick was leaning against the door leading out into the hallway, his arms crossed, waiting.

From the look on his face Dani knew that she had never before needed such a facile tongue and a quick brain to save her from his wrath.

Chapter Two

Dani would never forget the day she first saw Nicholas Montgomery. Her family had moved over a thousand miles from the place she'd been born in order for her father to accept a promotion and substantial pay raise. Both her mother and father had tried to explain to the five-year-old why they had moved, but all Dani knew was that she was no longer living near the grandmother who had always been there for her, or the cousins with whom she had shared many a happy hour. Never had she felt so alone.

On that particular day Dani sat on the front steps of her parents' home wishing for someone to play with, someone who knew her, someone who cared.

"Why are you crying?"

Dani hadn't seen anyone around her, and the voice startled her. She wiped her eyes and looked up, right into the sun. The figure standing there in silhouette seemed to glow, the light shimmering all around him. She squinted her eyes.

He was considerably older than she was, she knew that much. And he was tall. But what she noticed most of all was his golden blond hair. She'd never seen hair that color before, especially on a boy. It looked almost white in the sunlight.

When he stepped closer she was able to see his face more clearly and what she saw in his eyes surprised her. He seemed concerned about her, as though he really cared that she was sitting there alone, crying.

"Did you hurt yourself?" he asked when she merely stared at him without saying anything.

She shook her head and dried her eyes with the back of her hand.

He sat down on the step just below her so that his eyes were on her level. "What's your name?"

"Dani."

"Dani? Like in Daniel?"

"Danielle."

"That's a pretty name. My name is Nick." He glanced toward the door. "Is this your house?"

She nodded.

"You haven't lived here long, have you?"

She shook her head.

"I didn't think so." He pointed to the house next door. "I live over there."

She looked at the white two-story house in silence.

"Do you go to school?"

She shook her head.

He smiled at her and Dani knew that she had never seen such a warm, friendly smile before. "You don't talk much, do you?"

"Sometimes my mom says I talk all the time."

"Did she tell you not to talk to strangers?"

She nodded.

"Then you're being very smart not to talk with me." He stood, walked over to the door and rang the door- bell. Dani watched in astonishment as Nick introduced himself and explained that he was looking for work for the summer and would like to keep their lawn mowed. He chatted with her mother as though they were equals, explained that his mother worked afternoons but that he was certain she would like to get to know her new neighbors.

Most astonishing of all, he asked if he could take Dani down to the corner and buy her an ice-cream cone, and maybe introduce her to some of the neighborhood kids who played in the park another block away.

Dani's mother decided to go with them, so the three of them spent the afternoon together with Nick introducing both of them to the neighbors.

By the time they returned home Dani was convinced that Nick was her guardian angel who had come to keep her company, to protect her and to guide her.

Nothing had happened in the ensuing years to cause her to change her mind.

Now she eyed him with more than a hint of wariness as he leaned against the door watching her. Her so-called guardian looked far from angelic at the moment.

"Nick, do you have a shirt I could borrow to sleep in?" He continued to stare at her. "Or, I could just sleep in my sweatshirt." She turned back to the bathroom.

"Look in the second drawer over there," he said, nodding toward a chest of drawers. She followed his instructions and discovered a treasure trove of older clothing. Dani quickly grabbed a sweatshirt left over from his college days and pulled it over her head. The hem fell almost to her knees. She slipped the towel from around her body.

"This is great. Thank you."

Slowly he straightened until he was standing fully upright in the doorway. "Come into the den. We need to talk." With that ominous ultimatum, Nick disappeared down the hallway.

Dani looked toward the empty door. He was really angry with her this time. Would it help if she apologized for showing up on his doorstep unannounced?

Yet she'd done exactly that many times in the past and he'd never been quite this hostile. But then, she realized, she hadn't done something like this in a long time. Since she'd graduated from college, Dani had focused all her energy on her career. Getting a position in the research-and-development department of Merrimac Industries had seemed like a miracle. The semiconductor industry was exciting and she especially enjoyed looking for new and better ways to improve the product.

"Dani! Get down here!"

The sound of Nick's voice pierced her reverie and she gave a start. How was she going to explain to him what she had discovered, since all of the information was highly confidential?

She forced herself to retrace her earlier path and return downstairs. He stood waiting for her in the hallway. As soon as she appeared at the top of the stairs he turned away and strode into the den.

"This had better be good," he warned when she walked through the doorway. "I'd thought you had outgrown your trick of pretending to be a child just because you're sometimes mistaken for one."

"I'm sorry, Nick. No one has treated me that way in a long time and I guess I fell into my routine out of habit."

"Sit down," he said, waving to a chair. He walked over to the bar and poured himself a drink. "Do you want something?"

She shook her head, then realized he wasn't looking at her. "No, thank you."

After he dropped a couple of ice cubes in the glass he walked over to the sofa and sat down.

"What's all this about?"

She stared into his eyes and wished they didn't look so hard, so unforgiving. Never in her life had she been in more need of some understanding.

"As you know, I've been working at Merrimac Industries for the past two years—"

"How would I know that?" he asked, interrupting her attempt to get her thoughts in some sort of order.

She didn't hide her surprise. "I thought your mother might have mentioned it."

He sighed, running his hand through his already rumpled hair. "This may come as a shock to you, Danielle, but you aren't the main topic of my conversations with my mother.''

They both knew that their mothers had always hoped the two of them would marry someday, an attitude that Nick had always found more than a little irritating.

''Well, it really doesn't matter. The thing is that I work in a very security-sensitive area. I have been dating one of my coworkers for the last few months and—''

''Isn't that a little stupid, Dani?''

''What do you mean?''

''Haven't you ever heard that office romances can create innumerable problems?''

''No. I wish somebody had mentioned it. Then maybe I wouldn't be in this mess.''

''All right. So what's happened? You had a fight and now you can't—''

''No, darn it! That isn't it. If you would stop interrupting me maybe I could tell you what's happened. Sometimes your writer's imagination drives me crazy. You can always come up with some idea that no one else would think of.'' She paused, narrowing her eyes. ''Maybe that's what I'm hoping you'll do now.''

He leaned back on the sofa and propped his feet on the coffee table, his hands behind his head. When he didn't say anything more, she continued.

"I think I first got suspicious of Frank when I was over at his apartment one evening and the phone rang. He sounded strange, explained he couldn't talk. At first I thought it was another woman and didn't think much about it. We're more friends than anything else. But then I noticed that he's been jumpy lately in the lab. He was working on one of our new formulas the other day when I walked up. He immediately removed it from the screen as though I wasn't supposed to see it."

"What does all of that have to do with your barging in here tonight interrupting what was shaping up to be a very promising evening?"

"I'm coming to that. I decided to take a look at what Frank is working on, but I didn't want him to catch me, so I decided to return to the office tonight." When he didn't comment she went on, "I signed in with the guard and went to my office. I had made a recent printout of what we've been working on and discovered a couple of discrepancies in the figures from earlier notes. When I checked what Frank had been doing, I realized that he is subtly changing some of the formulas we're working with. The problem is, I don't understand why." She got up and began to pace. "I didn't know what to do with the information, but I wanted evidence, so I ran off copies of his work and hid them in my purse."

"Why did you have to hide them?"

"Because we're not allowed to take anything out of the office complex." She glanced around, then remembered that her purse was upstairs. "I stopped at the security guard's desk to sign out. He glanced into my purse in accordance with standard procedure, then handed my purse back to me. I'd almost reached the front door when he suddenly hollered at me." She paused in her pacing and stared at Nick. "Do you have any idea how scared I was? My heart was beating triple time and when he yelled I knew he must have realized he hadn't checked the side pocket. I broke and ran." She paused, taking a deep breath. "I jumped in my car and no sooner had I driven out of the gates than I saw a police car."

"My God, Dani, you're sounding totally paranoid. So what if you saw a police car? You hadn't done anything wrong."

She shook her head. "I thought maybe the guard had alerted them. I had planned to return to my apartment and try to decide what to do with the information I had, but when I saw the police, I panicked. I decided to come here."

"Did they follow you?"

"If they did, I think I lost them."

He shook his head.

"What does that mean?"

"I was just thinking that in the twenty years I've known you, you have invariably meant trouble in my life. Tonight doesn't seem to be any different."

"I resent that remark. I haven't always given you trouble."

"I suppose that's true. Sometimes you've just given me grief."

"Nick!"

"All right, all right. So what do you want from me?"

"A place to stay where I feel safe. I need to think about what to do next."

"There's nothing to think about. You turn what you know over to the authorities and let them deal with it."

"But who can I trust?"

"Oh, come on, Dani."

"No, I mean it. Frank is head of our department. If he's playing around with our figures, he's doing some sabotage that could destroy the company."

"So call the head of the company. Unless, of course, you've decided he's also behind this conspiracy." He finished off his drink and looked at her.

"You think I should contact Mr. Worthington?"

"What options do you have?"

"But he could fire me for disregarding procedures and bringing the papers home with me."

"Or he could decide you're Frank's accomplice and decide to send you to prison."

"Oh, dear God. I never thought of that."

Nick dropped his head back on the sofa and closed his eyes. Without opening them, he said, "The problem with you, Dani dearest, is you never think until you've acted."

She stood there in the middle of the room and glared at him, a completely wasted action since he still had his eyes closed. But somehow it made her feel better. He could be so insufferable at times. Why had she thought he would help her? Now that he was a big-shot playwright, consorting with movie stars and getting his name in the papers all the time, he didn't care what happened to her.

He opened his eyes and looked at her, then leaned toward her and held out his hand. "Come here."

She reluctantly walked over to him. He took her hand and tugged her down on the sofa beside him. After he draped his arm across her shoulder, he said, "You've had a very busy day. I would suggest that you go upstairs and get some sleep. In the morning we'll contact your Mr. Worthington and let him deal with all of this, all right?"

"Even if it means losing my job?"

"Consider your options. You could have kept your nose out of what was going on. You could have gone to work each day and minded your own business. Since you chose not to, you have to look at your next set of options. The company needs to know what's been happening."

She sat quietly for several minutes. Finally she sighed. "I suppose you're right."

"Of course I am.".

"You needn't sound so arrogant about it."

He smiled. "All right. I'm humbly aware of how right I am. Is that any better?"

"What do you think?"

He leaned over and kissed her on the cheek. "Go get some sleep."

She turned toward him and threw her arms around his neck. "I'm so sorry for interrupting your evening. I just didn't know where else to turn."

"You can't be any sorrier than I am, believe me."

"I'll make it up to you, I promise."

He unwrapped her arms from around him. "Why does a promise like that strike terror into my heart? Could it be I know you a little too well?"

His cool tone almost made her cringe. The invisible wall he had erected between them a few years ago was still in place, no matter what she did or said. Perhaps he'd never forgiven her for breaking up his engagement. A long list of possible reasons for why he'd distanced himself from her popped into her mind. Perhaps she'd do well to accept his behavior rather than to ask him for an explanation.

"There's no reason for anyone to know that I'm here, is there?" she asked.

"You mean other than Letitia?"

"She doesn't count. She considers me a child."

"Why do you ask?"

"I wouldn't want to cause you any more problems than I already have."

"Why is it you always have this attack of conscience immediately after you've managed to play havoc with my life?"

Dani moved away from him without answering. He certainly wasn't in the frame of mind to accept any form of apology from her. Perhaps he'd be in a better mood tomorrow.

She was almost at the doorway when she heard Nick say, "Pleasant dreams, Dani." The irony in his voice made her flinch.

It took Dani a long while to go to sleep that night. Her thoughts kept returning to what she had discovered earlier in the evening. Why would Frank be involved with something that would hurt the company he worked for? She could perhaps understand his actions if he appeared to be unhappy with his job and the opportunities for growth there.

He was a brilliant man with a future that would only become better as time passed. Why would he jeopardize what he had?

Dani turned over and buried her head in her pillow. Perhaps by morning she would feel better able to deal with her newfound knowledge and the fact that by uncovering what was happening she could somehow be implicated in whatever was going on.

Dani was awakened the next morning by the smell of fresh-brewed coffee. When she first opened her eyes she couldn't remember where she was and for a moment she felt a sense of panic.

Nick. Of course. She had spent the night at Nick's. Hurriedly she climbed out of bed and went into the bathroom. After washing her face and using the new toothbrush she'd found there, Dani dressed in the jeans and sweatshirt she'd had on the night before and went in search of her host.

She paused just inside the kitchen doorway. He was standing at the counter, his back to her, wearing a pair of jeans that should have been tossed in the trash a few years before. His feet and the upper half of his torso were bare.

Dani couldn't remember the last time she'd really looked at Nick—noticed the width of his shoulders or the way the muscles in his back caused his spine to form a slight hollow down its length.

He glanced over his shoulder and saw her standing there. From the dampness she noted in his hair, Dani decided he must have just gotten out of the shower.

"Coffee's ready if you want some," he said, moving away from the counter and sinking into one of the kitchen chairs.

"Thanks." She walked over to the coffeepot and poured herself a cup, then joined him at the table.

"So what do you intend to do?" he asked after a few moments of silence.

"Wake up."

Nick smiled. How could he have forgotten that Dani wasn't at her best in the morning? For all her sunny disposition, she did tend to be a little cranky during the first hours of the day.

"Do you plan to call your boss?"

She made a face. "I don't think I have much choice," she mumbled into her cup.

"Do you want to call him from here?"

She glanced up, startled. "I didn't think you wanted to be involved."

"It's a little late to consider my feelings, wouldn't you say?"

"I suppose."

He glanced at his watch. "Why don't you try him now before he's out on the golf course or somewhere?"

"I think you're looking forward to seeing me catch hell, aren't you?"

The look of innocence he gave her did not fool her for a minute. "You mean someone else might decide that your impetuous unprofessional behavior lacks something?"

"It must be wonderful to be perfect. You don't have to deal with your own faults and problems."

He sighed. "True. Very true."

Dani thought about throwing her cup at him but could quickly see that the momentary gratification would not be worth the consequences.

Nick watched as she reluctantly went over to the wall phone, thumbed through the phone book until she found a number, then dialed it. He unashamedly listened to her end of the conversation.

"Hello. This is Danielle Devereaux. I was wondering if I could speak with Mr. Worthington, please... Thank you." She turned and looked out the window, refusing to acknowledge Nick's presence in the room. "Hello, Mr. Worthington. I'm very sorry to bother you at home, but something has come up at the office that I really think you need to know about." She took a deep breath. "I'm really afraid that there's some industrial espionage going on in the research-and-development department."

Chapter Three

When Dani hung up the phone her face was white. "He's coming over here," she announced.

"Somehow I got that impression. It must have been when you gave him directions on how to find the place."

"Well, I didn't think we should be seen meeting in public."

"I see. Instead, you see yourself as some sort of heroine in a spy story, I take it."

She looked incensed. "Hardly. I probably won't have a job when I get through talking with him." She glared at Nick. "Aren't you going to get dressed?"

He glanced down at his bare chest. "The man isn't coming to visit me. You're the one who's managed to pique his curiosity."

"Nick, please don't be critical. As soon as we have our talk and I show him what I've found, we'll both leave you alone."

"Too bad you didn't think of that before you came crashing in here last night."

"Don't worry. I don't intend to include you in my life ever again."

Hours later Dani sat in the den staring across the room at Nick in shock. Her earlier declaration couldn't have been more wrong.

How could all of this have happened?

It had started when Mr. Worthington arrived. She had explained her suspicions to him, shown him the printouts and waited for him to respond.

His response had been unexpected. He asked if he could use the phone, excused himself and went into the other room. When he returned he explained that they would be joined shortly by a couple of F.B.I. agents.

As if that wasn't bad enough, once the government officials had been apprised of the situation, the three men began to discuss the strategy of the case.

"It's most important that you show no suspicions toward this Frank Dekin, Ms. Devereaux," the agent who had identified himself as Samuel Adams explained. "What we want to do is watch him, see who his contacts are and what's behind all of this. So you will need to behave in the same way toward him as you have in the past."

"You don't understand. I've been dating the man. There's no way I can continue to date him now that I know he's some type of industrial spy."

The two agents looked at each other. Then one of them said, "I suppose you could stop seeing him socially, if necessary."

"You mean just stop seeing him without giving him some type of explanation? Wouldn't that make him suspicious?"

"You could just explain to him that you've met someone else."

She looked at the man in disgust. "And what do I do when he sees that there's no man in my life?"

"What I'm saying here is that you start dating someone else."

"I don't know anyone else. Don't you understand? I work long hours and don't have time for a social life. That's one of the reasons Frank and I started seeing each other. We would end up working late, then stopping somewhere together for a late meal. After a while we began to go to social functions together. The relationship just sort of evolved.''

At that point in the conversation Mr. Worthington had asked about her relationship with Nick, who had introduced himself at the front door and had diplomatically disappeared into some other part of the house during their meeting.

When she explained to the men that Nick was a man she'd known since childhood because their families lived next door to each other, the agents had immediately asked him to join them in the den.

After outlining the situation to him, one of the agents asked Nick if he would have a problem with helping them out in this situation.

"I'm not sure that I can see what part I would play but I'll do whatever I can to help."

"What we have in mind is for you to pose as her new love interest for the next few weeks, until we have the chance to work on setting up surveillance and getting the necessary evidence to make an arrest."

The expression on Nick's face had made it clear that he would have to draw on all of his acting skills to perform such a feat.

Mr. Worthington suddenly spoke up. "Better yet, let's look at the rare opportunity we've been given to utilize their long-standing friendship.

The only reason she would be seeing him now would be if they had decided to make a commitment to one another. Have Dani arrive at work on Monday with an engagement ring. That should explain the situation well enough.''

That was when Dani went into shock. Her look of horror couldn't have been any less than the one that Nick wore, however.

"Now wait a minute. I didn't agree to any engagement," Nick pointed out.

"Of course not. This is all a setup. But it would explain the suddenness of her seeing someone else. Perhaps all you need to do is pick her up after work, meet Frank, pretend the necessary adoration, then disappear. I'm sure Ms. Devereaux can make up anything more that might be necessary."

Dani didn't know what to do. How in the world had the situation turned into a phony engagement? And with Nick, of all people.

"Maybe I can pretend I've met someone from out of town. Wouldn't that work?"

"Could you be convincing about not wanting to see him if Frank wants to continue to spend time with you?

"I don't know. I can't see why he would care."

The men looked at each other. "If you want to try it that way it's up to you."

She gave a sigh of relief. "Yes, I'd much prefer that." She smiled at Nick. "I know that you would much prefer not to be bothered by all of this."

He didn't respond to her. Instead he asked, "Is there going to be any danger to Dani?"

One of the agents replied, "We'll do everything we can to see that she is protected. At this point we have no idea how the man will react if he feels that his plans are not working out."

"Then I think Dani should give notice and leave."

"You can't be serious!" She came to her feet.

"Why take a chance on your being hurt?" he asked reasonably.

"Oh, sure. I'm just supposed to toss my career down the drain. No big deal."

"Don't be so dramatic, Dani. I'm only talking about the time that it will take them to get the evidence they need."

"But, Mr. Montgomery, we need Dani," Adams pointed out quietly. "She's vital at the moment because she's on the inside, working with him. She can keep an eye on what is happening. She will recognize whenever he does anything not part of their routine." The agent's tone was polite and reasonable. And very determined.

"In that case, I'd prefer to be a part of it, even if I'm only on the fringes." He glared at Dani as though daring her to argue with him.

What difference did it make to him if it was dangerous or not? She couldn't understand his behavior. Sometimes she thought that Nick enjoyed being contrary just to keep her confused.

By the time Mr. Worthington and the agents left, Dani felt exhausted. She stood in the hallway watching as Nick escorted them to the front door. When he closed it behind them she said, "I guess I'd better be going home."

"I don't know about you, but I'm hungry. Why don't we go have lunch somewhere first?"

He sounded like the Nick who had always looked after her and for a moment she forgot the unease that had steadily grown inside her as Nick and the agents discussed the situation.

"I'm really sorry about all of this," she offered.

He dropped his arm around her and hugged her against him. "Don't worry about it. This should only take a few days, maybe a couple of weeks at the most." He took her hand and spread the fingers across his palm. "We've got to do something about a ring. Why don't we go look after lunch?"

"I don't think that's a good idea."

He walked her toward the door, opened it, then closed it behind them. "We'll talk about it after lunch."

The problem with Nick was he invariably got his own way.

The restaurant he chose for lunch was filled with light and abundantly blooming greenery. Dani immediately loved it. She glanced around at the bustling waitresses, the chattering diners and smiled. "Do you come here often?" she asked after they were seated and handed menus.

"Whenever I get tired of eating at home," he said, studying the menu.

"I wish you had let me go home first to change clothes. This isn't exactly my idea of luncheon attire." She glanced down ruefully at her sweatshirt and tattered jeans.

"You look fine."

Since he hadn't glanced up from the menu she made a face at him. "How would you know? You never look at me."

He raised his head and stared at her. "What a stupid thing to say. How would I know it was you if I didn't look at you?"

Nick met her black-eyed gaze, noting the thick fringe of dark lashes and the way her eyes tilted ever so slightly upward at their outer edges. Her creamy complexion looked as young as it had the day he first set eyes on her. She still had the same tiny nose with a short upper lip, the full lower lip curving enticingly to meet it. The dimple in her chin was still intact. Her short curls lay in wisps, framing her face and ears.

Of course he looked at her. He often saw her in his dreams.

As soon as they gave their order Nick leaned forward and picked up her hand. "What size ring do you wear?"

"I don't know. I never wear one."

He sighed. "Why is nothing ever simple with you?"

"Who wants to be considered simple?" she asked with a smile.

"All right. I'll concede the point. What kind of ring would you like to wear?"

"Nick. I just told you. I don't wear rings."

"You're going to for the next week or so." She heard his no-nonsense tone, the one he used when he was prepared to do battle to get his own way.

"Why are you insisting on this? The other men agreed we didn't have to go to such lengths to convince Frank."

"I don't want to take any chances. When he sees the ring he'll know there's no way a fiancé is going to tolerate your seeing another man."

She eyed him doubtfully. "Maybe, but personally I don't think he's going to be brokenhearted over the loss of an occasional date with me."

"I don't buy that. He's just probably been taking his time softening you up."

Her delighted laugh cascaded through the restaurant, causing several patrons to glance around and smile at her obvious enjoyment.

"Have it your way, then," she said with a shrug. "I'm not going to fight with you."

"Well, that's certainly a switch. You can't imagine how relieved I feel."

His slow smile caused a fluttery feeling somewhere in the vicinity of her stomach, and she glanced around to see if their food was coming. She must be hungry.

After lunch they went to a local jewelry store and Nick insisted on looking at all the rings it had. He began to see the problem as Dani goodnaturedly tried on different ones, only to have her tiny fingers seem to disappear beneath the setting.

And then he saw what he wanted. A delicately sculpted lily with a tiny pearl in its center appeared as dainty as she was. When he slipped it on her finger he knew that this was the one. It fit perfectly.

"I'll take it," he said, handing a charge card to the smiling salesman.

Dani had seen the price. "Are you sure?"

"Of course I'm sure. I know it isn't a traditional engagement ring but it reminds me of you."

She glanced down at the ring. It was beautifully made and she could almost see tiny little fairylike workmen forming the petals and placing the pearl in its proper space. She looked up at him, her eyes shining. Impulsively she threw her arms around his neck. "Thank you, Nick." She hugged him, placing a kiss on his chin.

By the time they got back to his house it was after four. "I really need to go home," she said, glancing at her watch. "I have all my weekend chores to do, grocery shopping, the works."

"Then I'll see you Monday. I'll pick you up at work and meet Frank."

"You won't be able to go into the lab. They'll call me from the front desk. I'll have to meet you there."

"So how do I meet him?"

"Is it really necessary that you do?"

"You'd better believe it."

She stared at him, wishing she could understand him better. "All right. I'll work something out."

He walked her to her car. "Try not to offend any police on the way home."

She opened the door to the car and laughed up at him. Suddenly he gathered her in his arms. "Take care of yourself, Tiny Tot," he said in a gruff voice, using a name he hadn't called her in years. Then he kissed her.

Nick had kissed her a few times in her life, casual brotherly kisses. However, this kiss was neither casual nor brotherly. He wrapped his arms around her tightly so that she could scarcely get her breath. Or maybe she had forgotten to breathe. He seemed to want to claim possession of her as he thoroughly explored her mouth. He nibbled at her bottom lip, ran his tongue over her upper lip, then slipped his tongue between them.

Dani lost track of where they were or possible reasons for why Nick had swept her into his arms. She was staggered by her reaction to his embrace.

This was Nick, a man she'd known most of her life. This was Nick, her friend. Nick, her protective guardian. And yet he was kissing her like Nick, her lover.

And she was allowing it. In fact she was reveling in all the new sensations that were busily sweeping through her.

By the time he relaxed his grip and allowed her to come up for air, they were both breathless.

The slight breeze had ruffled his hair, causing it to fall rakishly across his forehead. The burning light in his eyes as he stared down at her shook her as much as the kiss had. Dani forced herself to take a deep breath, hoping it was only the lack of oxygen that seemed to make the ground spin unsteadily beneath her feet. Dear God, what was happening to her?

Neither one of them said a word. Dani sank into the driver's seat and Nick carefully closed the door behind her. She pulled out of the driveway and gave a little wave before she headed toward her apartment.

Nick watched her drive away, his hands in his pockets.

Whatever had possessed him to kiss her? he wondered, perplexed by his unusual behavior. Granted, he was worried about her. As usual she'd managed to get herself into another scrape through her own impulsive need to understand anything that puzzled her. He shook his head and turned toward his home. Dani needed a keeper, that was for sure. He wondered if she understood the seriousness of what she'd gotten herself involved in this time. The F.B.I., for God's sake.

Dani Devereaux would be the death of him yet.

Chapter Four

"I really don't think this is a very good idea, Nick," Dani said once again as they rode the elevator to the top floor of the luxurious Manhattan condominiums.

Nick had been watching the numbers flicker ever higher on the panel, his hands stuck in the pockets of his tuxedo. He glanced at the diminutive woman standing beside him, dressed like the angel who generally perched at the top of his family's Christmas tree.

Her gown was made of some gauzy white material, shot through with threads of glittering silver. The top was strapless, cupping her breasts and molding her tiny waist, then flaring into a full skirt that fell to her toes. All she needed was a wand and maybe a halo to complete the illusion.

"I've already told you, Dani. This party was planned weeks ago. As the guest of honor, I'm obligated to attend."

"I know that, Nicky! What I'm saying is that there is absolutely no reason for me to go with you. I can't imagine why you insisted."

They reached the penthouse level and silently the door opened. "Because I don't like the idea of leaving you in Connecticut at night on your own."

"Oh, for God's sake, Nick. I've lived alone for years."

"But not with someone like Frank lurking about."

"For your information, Frank does not lurk. He's totally harmless. I dated him for almost three months before this investigation began."

"He didn't seem harmless to me. Besides, look at what he's doing."

She glanced up at him in disgust. "He's a possible spy, Nick. Not a rapist."

"How would you know? How many rapists have you known personally?"

They paused in front of a double door. "Honestly, Nick. You're worse than my parents at hovering and worrying. Is it something in the genes or do you train for that sort of thing?''

He rang the doorbell without looking at her. ''There's no reason to take any chances. By next week this whole thing should be over with, two weeks max.''

''So in the meantime you're going to insist on dragging me around with you wherever you go?''

At last he looked down at her. ''Why not? It keeps you out of mischief.''

''But I don't fit in with your friends, Nick.''

''They aren't my friends. They're business associates.''

''I never know what to say to them.''

''You know how to listen and that is an invaluable trait, believe me. They're going to love you.''

Before she could rebut his last statement the door opened and they were engulfed in the party atmosphere.

Sometime later Dani found herself standing near the ornate fireplace, surrounded by faces that she'd seen in magazines and newspapers, and a couple that had appeared on television more than once.

Where was Nick? she thought helplessly, while she nodded and smiled at the young man who was so earnestly explaining how tough it was to

find a decent agent to represent him on the West
Coast. Her gaze scanned the room.

Ah, there he was. Three men stood talking to
him. One of them had a tall redhead clinging to
his arm and Dani wondered if the man had any
idea how he was tempting fate to wave such a
morsel in front of Nick. Tall redheads were his
specialty. She almost made a face at the thought.
Small brunettes never caught his eye. If she
hadn't known him for years she doubted if he'd
ever have paid any attention to her.

Tonight was a perfect example. They had become separated not long after they arrived, their
host dragging Nick off to meet some potential
backers for a play he was currently working on.

Not that Dani wasn't proud of Nick and his
success. It was just that they were so different.
This wasn't her scene at all. All the glitter and
glamour of show business left her cold. No matter how hard she tried, she couldn't convince
herself that these people were real. They were always playing a part, even at a party.

Take Gavin Gray, the young man who was
busy monopolizing the conversation at the moment. She would bet her next week's salary that
every gesture, every expression he made, had
been carefully practiced in front of a mirror to
insure he projected the proper image.

He leaned toward her, placing the palm of his hand against the wall next to her head.

"Have you ever been to California, Danielle?"

She shook her head, wondering how she had allowed herself to become trapped.

"I'm going out next week. If you'd like, maybe we could—"

"There you are, darling," Nick inserted smoothly, somehow managing to extricate Dani without looking obvious. "It's good to see you again, Gavin," he said with a nod. "I hope you don't mind, but there's someone I want Dani to meet."

Gavin broke out into a scintillating smile. "Not at all. I understand completely."

Dani thought she heard Nick mutter something beneath his breath but she wasn't certain. As soon as they were out of earshot he said, "I didn't mean to abandon you like that."

"It's all right."

"No, it isn't. I just got caught up in talking business and didn't realize how the time had slipped away, and you with it."

"Who did you want me to meet?"

"There wasn't anyone. I just wondered if we shouldn't try the buffet. It looks delicious."

She glanced up at him in surprise and he gave her a wicked smile, the one he used to wear when he managed to successfully play hooky and had to brag about his exploits to her. She didn't trust that smile. Not one bit.

By the time they left the party all Dani wanted to do was get her shoes off. Getting dressed up had been fun because it was something that she rarely did. Her life was set in a fairly staid routine—going to parties with famous people, even if he happened to be the neighbor she'd grown up with, was not part of her daily life. She would just as soon keep it that way.

As soon as they reached the car, she slipped her shoes off, set the seat back and relaxed, closing her eyes.

"Going to sleep?"

"Unless you want me to stay awake to keep you company."

He chuckled and, reaching over, placed a cassette into the tape deck. "No, that would be above and beyond your call of duty." He adjusted the volume of the soft seductive music. "I want to thank you for going with me. I really hate those things, but I found myself actually enjoying being there with you."

"Will wonders never cease," she murmured. "You used to carry on something awful whenever I tried to go with you anywhere."

"Let's face it. I was considerably younger then."

"But I've seen no evidence that your attitude has changed over the years."

"Maybe I'm mellowing with old age."

She grinned and closed her eyes. "That will be the day."

Dani allowed her thoughts to drift back over the past week. She'd felt foolish when she arrived at work Monday morning and the security guard on duty explained that the night security guard had left a note with her identification badge, saying she had dropped it when she was there Friday evening.

So that was why he had called her. Like an idiot she had run from him. As for the police, she still wasn't sure whether or not they saw her or had, in fact, tried to pursue her.

If it hadn't been for Mr. Worthington and the two agents, she would have decided that she had imagined everything that had happened. But the information she had shown Mr. Worthington had proved her right to be concerned about Frank and what he was doing.

She had been very nervous when she walked into the lab, but Frank had treated her the same as he always did and she had gradually relaxed with him. They were both busy all day and it wasn't until her phone rang and she was told that Nick Montgomery was there to see her that she glanced at her watch and realized it was almost six o'clock.

Frank was still working. She decided that she might as well get this over with.

"Frank, do you have a minute?"

He glanced up from his notes, peering through his thick-lensed glasses. "Sure, Dani. What's up?"

"I was getting ready to leave and—"

He glanced at his watch. "I didn't realize how late it was." He frowned. "I can't leave this where it is at the moment, but if you'll give me about another half hour..."

"Uh, Frank. There's someone I want you to meet. He's waiting in the lobby for me."

"He?" Frank asked stiffly.

She could see him tense. "Yes."

He came to his feet. "What are you trying to tell me, Dani?"

She held up her hand, never so glad to be wearing the ring as she was now. Somehow it made the lie more palatable. "I became engaged over the weekend."

Frank paled and Dani knew how he must be feeling, because the sense of betrayal when she discovered what he was doing in their department had hit her in the same way.

"Engaged! But you haven't been seeing anyone but me. I don't understand."

She started toward the door. "I'll explain as we go." She opened the door. "You see, Nick Montgomery and I grew up together."

"Nick Montgomery. The playwright?"

"Yes."

"You're engaged to Nick Montgomery?"

She grew a little exasperated. "That's what I'm trying to tell you." Frank was staring at her as though he'd never seen her before. What was the matter with him? Was he shocked to find out that she even knew Nick? Not that she could blame him, she supposed. After all, she'd never mentioned his name before.

She should have known Nick would have been prepared to play his part. As soon as they reached the lobby, he swept Dani into his arms and gave her a kiss that was both intimate and thorough. When he finally raised his head he murmured, "I've missed you today," in such a way that the receptionist and Frank would think they had spent the entire weekend in bed together!

"Uh, Nick, I'd like you to meet Frank Dekin. Frank and I work in research and development."

"Good to meet you, Frank," Nick said in a hearty voice. "Dani's spoken of you."

"Has she?" Frank asked, looking over at Dani as though wondering what she had said. "You have the advantage, then. Dani's never mentioned you to me.''

"Frank and I have been friends since shortly after I came to work here,'' she explained a little nervously. Frank wasn't taking this situation the way she had expected.

His look was accusing. "I would have said we've been much more than friends.''

Nick kept his arm around her, his possession evident. "I can understand that. I've known Dani since she was five years old. She's really special, isn't she?''

"Yes, she is.'' Frank glanced over at Dani, then back at Nick, shaking his head slightly. "I had no idea she even knew you.''

Nick smiled. "I'm not at all surprised. You see, we had one hell of a fight a couple of years ago. Since that time I lost track of her. A few days ago I happened to run into her again and I realized what had been missing in my life, what I'd given up.'' The look he gave Dani would have melted steel at ten paces. "I decided not to let her slip away from me again.''

Frank glanced at Dani. "Doesn't sound as though he gave you much choice.''

Oh, dear. Now what could she say? She couldn't act worth a darn. Frank would recognize a lie immediately, which was why she'd been afraid to spend much time with him now that she had discovered what he was doing.

Before she could speak, Nick said, "You're absolutely right. I gave her no choice whatsoever. I counted on the fact that she loved me and always had, and that it was only her pride that had kept us apart."

Great. Now Nick was portraying her as immature and easily swayed. But what difference did it make, as long as Frank was convinced the engagement was real?

Frank had not taken his eyes off Dani while Nick spoke. "Is this what you want, Dani?"

She could only nod.

"Then I'm happy for you." He checked his watch. "Well, unless I intend to spend the night here I've got to get back to work." He nodded at them. "Glad to meet you, Montgomery. I've enjoyed your plays." His gaze met Dani's. "I'll see you in the morning."

"Yes."

Now, as she rode beside Nick back to Connecticut, she relived that meeting. The combination of the ring and Nick's enthusiastic embrace had seemed to convince Frank that Dani had chosen Nick. What could he say, after all? She and Frank had never talked about a relationship. Most of their conversations had been about work. They had found some similar tastes.

What they had was a comfortable friendship, or at least that was what it had been for Dani until she had begun to grow suspicious of Frank.

She had turned sideways in her seat with her legs curled up. Now she opened her eyes and studied Nick's profile while he drove. He looked devastating in black, his blond hair appearing even brighter in contrast. She had always found him attractive. He was like a rock she always knew was there, one she could depend on to help her. Once again he was helping her, but she was having a more difficult time accepting him in her life now.

She was older now and had become fairly self-sufficient over the years. If she hadn't panicked Friday night she would have gone home, slept on the problem, and no doubt by morning would have come to the same conclusion that Nick had reached: to contact Mr. Worthington. Had she done that, Nick would never have been involved.

Instead he was now her so-called fiancé, although he had not introduced her that way at the party earlier. Those were not the people who needed to know what was happening. If anyone had noticed her ring, no comments were made.

She glanced down at the ring on her finger. It was truly beautiful. Nick had convinced her that it was hers to wear even after this farce of an engagement was over. She would treasure it, she knew, because it had come from Nick.

Had there ever been a time when, in her girlish imaginings, she had pictured marrying Nick Montgomery one day?

Surely not. For one thing, Nick had made it clear that although he was willing to help her from time to time, on a daily basis he found her to be a great nuisance. It was hard to get romantic over someone who treated you in such a fashion.

For another, Dani had always known that she wasn't the type of woman, physically or emotionally, who attracted Nick. He liked the women in his life to be emotionally cool, calm and somewhat aloof. Dani knew herself well enough to know that she emotionally leaped into every new situation and got totally involved, sometimes over her head, which was why he'd had to figuratively wade in and save her on more than one occasion.

She thought she was over that, yet once again Nick had managed to help her out. But this was going to be the very last time, she vowed. No matter what happened to her in the future, she was determined to handle it without Nick's help.

Dani must have fallen asleep because the next thing she knew Nick was holding her in his arms and carrying her to her apartment door.

She stirred, trying to awake.

"I need your key," he said in a low voice. She felt the vibration of his words in his chest where she rested her cheek.

"My purse." She discovered that her purse hung by its tiny strap from the fingers that held her shoulders. She reached for it and found the key. When he leaned down, she stuck it in the lock and turned, and he pushed his weight against the door.

She flipped on the switch and looked up at him. "You can put me down now."

He grinned at her and obligingly allowed her feet to touch the floor. "It's kinda fun to carry you around like I did when you were a kid. I don't think you weigh much more now than you did then. The women I'm generally with would break my back if I tried sweeping them off their feet."

"I'm so pleased that I offer you some type of amusement," she responded wryly.

He laughed and pulled her into his arms. "I've missed you, Dani. The funny thing is I didn't even realize it until you came back into my life."

"I know. You missed me like a toothache."

"If anyone had asked me that's probably what I would have told them. But it isn't true. You have a way of making me stay honest with myself. You've never been overly impressed with my accomplishments, you've never allowed me to take myself too seriously, you've always wielded the pin that could burst my balloon of self-importance."

She looked up at him doubtfully. "I'm not certain whether to take that as a compliment or a complaint."

"Let's just say that I'm glad you came to me when you needed help this time."

She shook her head. "I was thinking about that on the way home tonight. If I hadn't become so paranoid I would have had no reason to bother you at all." She looked away from him. "I'm really sorry about messing up your weekend with Letitia."

When he didn't respond she forced herself to look up at him. He wore a very startled expression on his face.

"I just realized that I had forgotten about Letitia with all that's been happening this past week."

"How could you forget her? She's beautiful. She's everything you've always admired in a woman."

"I know. And I've spent the last year pursuing her," he said in a strange tone.

"You don't suppose you're coming down with some dreaded disease, do you?" she asked anxiously. "I mean, how could you have forgotten—unless maybe some of your brain cells are blinking out and going to sleep.''

''All right, Dani, you don't need to make it sound as though I've slipped over the edge to senility. It's just that I've had a lot on my mind, that's all.''

She started to step out of his embrace but he tightened the hold. ''I'm sorry. I didn't mean to offend you.''

''I'm not used to your contrite side, Dani. It doesn't really fit your personality.''

She pointedly looked at her watch. ''Do you realize what time it is?''

''I know. Time to get some rest.'' He glanced around the apartment. ''I could stay here, couldn't I, rather than drive the extra thirty miles home?''

''You could, I suppose, but you won't get much rest. You'd have to sleep on the couch and Muffin will spend that time tromping up and down your torso in a sort of feline massage.''

''Muffin? Are you telling me you still have that mangy cat I found years ago?''

She pulled away from him and crossed her arms. ''He was not mangy. He was just hungry, cold and dirty.''

''And he'd been in a couple of losing battles.''

"So? He wasn't trying to win any beauty contests. He just wanted to live."

He glanced around the room. "Where is he?"

"Probably asleep on my bed. But don't think he wouldn't discover you if you decided to stay."

"It was just a thought. I've got some work I want to get done early in the morning, anyway." He glanced around the room once more. "You're sure you don't mind being alone?"

"What are you going to do if I say no? Hire me a bodyguard?"

"You may find all of this very funny, but we don't know how this man is going to react once he realizes he's under suspicion."

"There's no reason for him to come after me."

"You don't think he'll guess that you were the one who turned him in?"

She shivered. That thought had occurred to her more than once as she'd lain awake in the middle of the night. But she always managed to argue her way around it. She found it irritating that Nick had voiced her secret fear. Consequently she answered him somewhat brusquely. "Frank isn't the violent type, Nick. He wouldn't harm me."

"So you say." He took a couple of steps over to her and stroked her cheek with his finger. "I don't know why I worry about you. It must be a habit left over from childhood."

"I'll be fine. I don't think any of this was truly necessary. There was no reason for you to become involved."

"But I am." He leaned down and kissed her.

She swayed and he placed his hands on her shoulders, then slipped his arms around her once again.

Nick didn't understand what was happening to him. He didn't want to leave her. Her teasing and tormenting had made his teenage years hideously embarrassing. Had anyone asked, he would have assumed that to be anywhere where Dani Devereaux wasn't would be an ideal place to be.

So why did he want to be around her more and more? Why did he find excuses to call her, to spend time with her, to hold her, to kiss her?

Maybe Dani was right. Senility must be catching up with him.

Chapter Five

The noisy jangle of the telephone brought Dani out of a deep sleep. She fumbled for the receiver and managed to get it to her ear.

"H'lo," she mumbled, still more than half asleep.

"I want to thank you for sharing all of your wonderful news with your dad and me, Danielle. I mean, we recognize that we're nothing special in your life now that you've left home. Why should we expect to hear about the momentous things happening in your life?"

With her eyes still closed, Dani muttered, "Mornin', Mom."

"How could you do this to us, Dani? You knew how excited Mona and I would be. How could you let us learn about—"

Dani's eyes snapped open. She was awake. Oh, boy, was she ever awake. At the mention of Nick's mother's name she had an ominous feeling that catastrophe had struck.

"Mona? What exactly does Mona have to do with this phone call?"

"As if you didn't know. I'm certain that Mona is every bit as upset with Nick as we are with you. To have to learn that her son is getting married from an article in the newspaper when a simple phone call would have prepared her for the news. It's quite a shock I assure you."

"Nick is getting married?" she asked, suddenly worried about the story they had concocted. "It's in the papers that Nick is getting married?"

"Of course it is. With pictures and everything but quotes from the happy couple."

"Mom, how could I have told you? I didn't know that Nick—wait a minute." She sat up in bed, trying to think. "Mom, tell me what's in the paper."

"Just that my daughter and Mona's son saw fit to become engaged to each other, caring so little about their mothers' feelings they didn't bother to tell us first. Instead they let us read about the engagement in the Sunday supplement!''

"Oh, my God," she whispered, trying to picture all of the ramifications of such a development. "What sort of pictures?" she finally asked.

"There's one in a restaurant where he's holding your hand and you are both smiling. There's a picture of the two of you leaving a jewelry store together, and there's one of you dressed up in formal wear stepping out of a car while Nick is standing there looking totally besotted.''

A restaurant? The jewelry store? What was happening here? Had they been followed? She realized her mother was still talking and Dani forced herself to listen.

"It says, and I quote, 'Nick Montgomery, famous playwright with two successful plays currently running on Broadway, kept his current love under wraps by escorting Letitia Link to the recent opening of his newest play.''' She paused. "There's a picture of the two of them at the opening, by the way.'' Then she continued reading, " 'It was obvious to this reporter that Letitia was only a cover for the publicity-shy playwright's romance with his newest love. Although no formal announcement has been made, the sparkling ring on her left hand and the looks the two shared have convinced those who know him that Nick Montgomery has decided to end his bachelor days. The question, Nicky, is when?' ''

Dani couldn't think of anything to say. She sat there feeling numb, wondering if Nick had seen the morning paper.

"Is this true, Dani? I mean, it's hard to deny that you're the woman in those pictures, even though they don't give your name. And they printed a magnified picture of your hand, showing a ring. And from both your expressions, you certainly are enjoying each other."

"Mom, it's a long story and I don't really want to go into it at the moment."

"I see. Now you have to have secrets from your family. You don't trust us anymore, is that it? Or maybe you're ashamed of us now that Nick is so famous."

"Oh, Mother, that's not true and you know it. The fact is that you just woke me up and I'm not ready to sit here and try to explain what's happening. I'll call you back later."

With that she hung up the phone. Before her mother could call back she walked into the bathroom and turned on the shower.

Standing under the pulsing spray, Dani tried to decide what to do. How could she and Nick explain to whomever had written that article that what those pictures portrayed was an illusion?

No doubt her mother had exaggerated the way she and Nick had been looking at each other. Mothers always saw what they wanted to see, and her mother and Nick's mother would like nothing better than to have their offspring marry. She and Nick had made it clear years ago they were not interested in each other in that way, and she had hoped that her mother had forgotten her earlier dreams.

Obviously she hadn't, or she wouldn't have been so quick to call and give her a bad time.

What was she going to do? She wasn't in this by herself. She didn't dare tell her mother the truth, if for no other reason than that she and Nick were sworn to secrecy by the F.B.I.

The only thing she could think to do was go see Nick. Maybe he would have some thoughts on the subject. She hated to face him but she knew she had no choice.

As soon as she dried her hair and dressed, she grabbed her purse and keys. It would be better to get it over with, because she knew that before the day was out she would have to call her mother back and give her some kind of story.

She had no idea what.

Once again Dani ran to Nick for help.

After she rang the door bell for the third time Dani glanced at her wristwatch. It was a little after nine on Sunday morning. Nick hadn't left her place until after two o'clock. She made a face. Maybe she should have encouraged him to stay overnight at her place, even with Muffin's possible interference.

She turned away from the door. What could she do now? She hadn't realized how early it was once her mother had awakened her.

"What do you—Dani! Now why didn't it occur to me that it would be you at the door at such an ungodly hour?"

Nick had pulled on a pair of jeans; otherwise he'd come to door directly from bed. His hair stood up in peaks and he looked more than a little cranky.

"I'm sorry for coming over so early. I didn't realize—"

"I don't need to stand here listening to your excuses, Dani. Come inside. I need some coffee."

He shoved his hand through his hair and shook his head.

Why hadn't she thought things out a little better before dashing over to tell him, Dani wondered contritely as she followed him through the hallway and into the kitchen. She perched on one of the bar stools and watched as he measured out the coffee. Now that she was here she wasn't sure how to tell him what had happened.

She hadn't even bothered stopping to get a paper, which was rather stupid, since it was the newspaper article that had started this latest sequence of events. She slid off the bar stool and started toward the hall.

"Where are you going?"

"I forgot to get a paper. I'll be right back."

"Dani! If you think reading the Sunday funnies to me is going to put me in a better frame of mind, forget it. You might as well stay here and have a cup of coffee."

"I'll be right back," she said again, and hurried down the hallway. Maybe she had overreacted. It wouldn't be the first time. Maybe the article really hadn't been all that revealing. Once she looked at the paper she would decide whether to even tell him about it.

By the time she returned to the house, though, matters had been taken out of her hands. As soon as she walked back in Nick grabbed the paper and started rifling through it.

"I thought you didn't want to see the funnies."

He didn't look up. He found the Sunday supplement and threw the rest of the paper on the counter. He sat down on one of the stools and started thumbing through it.

She knew what he would find because she had already taken the time to glance at it. If anything, it was worse than what she had imagined. Why did people say that pictures never lied? This particular group of pictures were the most incriminating set of lies she'd ever faced.

Take the one, for instance, of them at the restaurant. Vaguely she remembered Nick taking her hand, but she was absolutely certain he had never looked at her with such warmth. But from the angle of the unknown photographer, the look on his face was of a man who had suddenly discovered paradise.

The one coming out of the jewelry store was just as bad. This time the photographer caught her gazing up at Nick and laughing. He held her hand and they looked for all the world like lovers without a care in the world.

But the one taken the night before stunned her. She remembered Nick's coming around the car and holding the door open for her. She remembered his taking her hand to assist her. But surely they hadn't been looking at each other as though they were the only two people in the world.

And yet neither one of them had seen a photographer. She was absolutely certain there had been no flash, but then the entrance to the condominium complex had been well lit, and the valet had parked the car for them.

On the one hand, they had accomplished what they set out to do. Frank would have no lingering doubt about their engagement. But on the other hand, Frank was the only one they had needed to convince, and the meeting the week before had seemed to do just that. Whenever they had spoken for the rest of the week the subject had been solely business.

She had monitored his work and had twice caught discrepancies in what they were doing by way of experiments and what he was placing on the computer. Now that she was aware of his actions it was easy enough to follow his progress. He made no effort to hide anything because there was no reason to do so. Typing one number in place of another one could easily be explained away as a typographical error if she were to point it out, but there was no reason from Frank's viewpoint for her to closely watch what he recorded. She was also recording her own figures because she was working on a different aspect of the same formula.

Dani glanced at Nick. He was staring at the pictures in the paper, stunned. She knew the feeling. She sipped her coffee while she watched him read the entire article. She knew when he finished. He stared at the pictures once again.

"How did you find out?" she asked when it was obvious that Nick was going to spend the rest of the day memorizing the article and pictures without saying a word to her.

"A friend called from New York offering his congratulations."

"How did you respond?"

"I thanked him. How did you want me to respond?"

"I don't know. I didn't have a clue what to say when Mother called and—"

"Your *mother* called?" He laid his forehead against his hand. "Oh, God."

"Did you think she wouldn't see it?"

He shook his head. "I hadn't gotten that far in my thoughts." He rubbed his eyes with the heels of his hands. "I need some more coffee."

She got up and walked over to the coffeepot, filled both their cups and sat back down.

"Thanks."

"Don't mention it. It's the least I could do."

He looked at her in surprise.

"Let's face it. This whole thing's my fault. If I hadn't come charging over here that night, none of this would have—"

"Dani," Nick said, interrupting her agitated apology, "nobody forced me into getting involved in this deal. It was my choice. I knew what I was doing."

"You didn't know that your mother and mine were going to read about it in the Sunday paper!"

"Well, of course not. I can't imagine why anyone would decide all of this was worth printing, much less reading about."

She looked at him in astonishment. "Because you're news, Nick. Haven't you gotten that through your head yet? People are fascinated by you. They want to know everything they can."

He shook his head. "It just doesn't make sense."

"Maybe not, but that's the way the world is."

"I mean, I could understand it if I'd invented something that was going to revolutionize the way we live, or discovered the cure for some nasty disease. But I haven't done anything but write some plays that people enjoyed."

"Like it or not, you've got to live with it now. You're a bona fide celebrity, and a celebrity doesn't have much claim to a private life anymore."

When he didn't say anything more she said, "So what are we going to tell them?"

"Who?" he muttered absentmindedly, still staring at the collection of pictures spread between his elbows.

"Nick, it might be a good idea for you to go for a senility check. I'm really beginning to worry about you. Our parents. That's who. My mother is demanding an explanation. She said your mother is upset because you didn't tell her a thing. We're sworn to secrecy. So what do we tell them?''

Nick slowly turned his head and looked at her. He stared at her for a long time. She felt as though his gaze touched her on every surface of her face—her eyes, her cheeks, her nose, her mouth, her chin. And as he gazed at her he lifted his hand and slid his fingers into the short curls above her ear.

''We tell them we're getting married,'' he finally said, just before his lips touched hers.

Chapter Six

Every time Nick kissed her, Dani lost her ability to hang on to coherent thought. Never had she needed that ability as much as now. What had he just said? What—

It was no use. His hand slipped behind her head, cupping it while he continued to kiss her with a familiarity that hadn't been there a couple of weeks before. The reactions within her had become instantaneous. As soon as his mouth touched hers, her head began to spin, her spine liquified and her heart jumped around like a frog in her chest.

When he finally raised his head, she could only stare at him with bemusement. She slowly managed to focus her gaze on his flushed face, and for the first time she realized that she was seeing the same look that had been captured by the photographer at the restaurant. "Nick?"

"Hmmm?"

"You can't be serious."

"About what?"

"You said that we're going to get married."

"No, I didn't. I said we'd tell our folks that we're going to get married. As soon as the authorities have enough evidence on Frank, we'll tell them we changed our minds."

She managed to take a shaky breath. "Whew. I can live with that."

He smiled. "I thought you could."

"You really scared me there for a moment."

"I noticed."

"I mean, the one thing that you and I could never do would be to get married. It would ruin a beautiful friendship."

His smile seemed a little wistful. "Would it?"

"You can't doubt it!" She got off the stool and paced the kitchen floor. "In the first place I'm not your type."

He cocked his head. "And what is my type?"

She waved her hand. "You know. The tall slinky redhead type—brainy and built."

"You're brainy, as you call it, and there's nothing wrong with your build."

She waved away his comments. "You've always considered me a pain in your life . . . a pest. I try your patience, remember?"

He nodded. "You do manage to do that with alarming regularity, I must admit."

She spun around and waved both arms at him. "So you can see how ridiculous it would be to try to convince our parents that we are actually planning to get married."

He stroked his chin and managed to hide his smile. "I see your point."

"Good. So what can we tell them?"

"Dani, like it or not, we've got to play along with the story for now."

Her bottom lip became more pronounced and he grinned when she said, "I don't like it."

"Yes, I can see that."

"I'm no good at lying."

"You never were."

"I don't like to lie. It goes against everything I believe in."

"Look at it this way," he said, as if trying to reason with her. "You aren't actually lying. We *are* engaged. You're wearing a ring to prove it."

"But—"

"An engagement is an announcement that a couple intends to marry. We both intend to marry—someday. Just not each other, right?"

She folded her arms. "I haven't gotten that far in my goals yet. I'm trying to get my career established first. After that, I might consider it."

"At least you haven't totally ruled out the possibility," he said.

She narrowed her eyes and asked, "Are you making fun of me?"

"How can you say that, Dani? Look, you came to me wanting help. I'm trying. It wasn't my idea to pretend to be engaged. I just went along with it."

Dani felt ashamed of herself for getting so upset with Nick. He was right of course. She had run to him for help and regardless of how he felt he always rescued her whenever she asked.

She plopped on the bar stool again. "So what do you think we should do now?"

He glanced at his watch. "Obviously we owe the folks some kind of explanation. Why don't we drive down to see them today? If you can come up with some other story besides the real one to explain our phony engagement, I'll go along with it."

"How about you were jilted and I caught you on the rebound?"

He shook his head. "Too corny."

"It happens all the time."

"It's still corny and frankly I don't think my mother would buy it."

Dani thought for a moment. "Mine would, but my dad knows you too well."

"Exactly."

"I mean, everyone knows how independent you are and that you never do anything that you don't want to do."

"Agreed."

"So." She stood up and began to pace again. "What if I tell them that I fell in love with this married man and— No, that would be even worse." She scratched her ear. "You're the writer—the one with all the imagination. Surely you can come up with something plausible."

He studied her for a brief moment before he said, "What if I tell them that after knowing you for twenty years I was suddenly struck by the fact that I love you more than I've ever loved anyone in my life? Realizing that, the only thing for me to do was to marry you before I lost you to another man."

She shook her head. "They'll never believe it."

"Why not?"

Dani grinned as she threw her arms out wide. "Because all of them know *me* too well!"

Nick unwound himself from his bar stool and walked over to her. His intent gaze pinned her to the spot. "You don't think anyone would be able to fall in love with you?"

"Of course I do," she explained patiently. "I'm certainly capable of attracting all sorts of love from various people. We're talking about you."

"Care to explain that one?"

"Come on, Nick. We've already gone into this. You find me too impulsive, too emotional, too—" she waved her hand "—everything. You want a woman who's very together. I'm working on it, but in my heart I know that whenever I get too emotional I won't be thinking very clearly and I'll do some pretty dumb things." She patted his cheek. "And whenever I do, you get irritated, aggravated or angry, depending on what I've done."

"That doesn't mean I don't love you."

She smiled as though she were dealing with a very young child. "I know that. And I love you, too. But that doesn't mean I want to marry you, or attempt to live with you for any length of time."

"You find me that difficult to get along with?"

"Well, let's face it. You're pretty much set in your ways. You like order and routine and I always manage to disrupt that part of your life."

"All right. You've managed to convince me. So let's go see our folks, okay?"

She smiled up at him, pleased that she had argued her case so effectively. "Do you plan on going barefoot and without a shirt?"

"Give me fifteen minutes." He turned around and walked out of the kitchen.

Dani busied herself washing their cups and straightening the kitchen. Nick could find some of the strangest topics of conversation sometimes. He enjoyed arguing just to see what she'd say, she decided. She wondered what he'd do if she suddenly announced that she fully intended to marry him. Boy, would he have howled in outrage.

She knew better than to try something like that. Nick did allow her a degree of latitude in baiting him, but she knew her limits. Of course he felt he had no limits as far as she was concerned.

He had succeeded in getting her mind off what they were going to tell her folks, anyway. Which reminded her that she needed to call her mom back.

She went over and picked up the phone.

The closer they got to Teaneck the more nervous Dani became. Part of it was because of the odd mood Nick was in. Looking relaxed and rested, he'd rejoined her where she waited for him in his den. His attitude was a far cry from the one he'd had when he'd answered the door earlier in the day.

They had gone in his car, leaving hers in his driveway, and he had whistled along with the music while Dani had mentally rehearsed possible rejoinders to their parents' anticipated comments.

By the time they pulled into her parents' driveway she was a nervous wreck.

Mona must have been watching for them because she was out the door of her house and throwing herself into Nick's arms as soon as he got out of the car.

"You're acting like you haven't seen me in years, Mom," he pointed out with a grin. "It's only been a couple of weeks."

Mona laughed. "I know. But I've missed you." She turned to Dani and gave her a massive hug. "And it's been much too long since I've seen you, Dani. How have you been?"

"Fine."

Mona lifted Dani's hand. "Oh, Dani, this is beautiful." She looked at Nick. "Did you pick this out?"

"We both did."

Mona's smile reminded Dani of Nick's. "I'm so proud of you two for finally realizing what the family has known for years. You've always been a daughter to me, anyway, Dani. Now it's going to be official.''

Dani's glance at Nick was a plea for help. He dropped his arm around his mother's shoulders. "Let's go face the music, Dani." He looked at his mother. "I understand Sarah is quite irate."

"We both are," Mona replied. "How could you two have made such an important decision and not shared it with us?"

"Because it isn't official yet," he said, winking at Dani.

"That ring looks pretty official to me."

They reached the door and were once again greeted with hugs, this time from Sarah and John Devereaux.

Sarah had to feed them immediately, which was a normal ritual in the Devereaux household. Then Nick had to catch John up on what was happening with his career. When Dani was asked about her job she answered in the most general terms and changed the subject.

They were having her mother's famous coconut cake and coffee when Mona asked, "So when's the wedding?" which caused Dani to choke on her bite of cake. Nick solicitously pounded on her back while her mother got her a glass of water.

When she finally stopped coughing and was busy wiping the tears from her eyes, Nick responded.

"That's why we're here."

Dani gave a quick sigh of relief, only to realize she'd breathed too soon. With something akin to horror Dani heard Nick say, "We wanted your help in planning the wedding. I know how long you've each waited for us to marry. Now you can work together on the same project. See how much time and money that will save everyone?"

Everyone laughed. Everyone except Dani, that is. Dani stared at Nick as though he's suddenly begun to speak in a foreign language.

"I take it that since you've waited most of your lives, you're ready to have a short engagement."

Before Dani could contradict her father, Nick took her hand and squeezed it—hard—while he said, "The sooner the better."

Her gasp of outrage and pain was muffled beneath the comments that little bomb set off.

"If that means what it sounds like..." John began.

Nick laughed. "No, no. Nothing like that. You're not going to have to drag out your shotgun or anything."

"Nick!" Both Dani and Mona looked at him in shock.

Nick shrugged. "That's what he was thinking. I was just trying to reassure him. My darling Dani is as pure as the driven snow and I intend to see that she remains that way." His grin was pure wolf. "At least until after the wedding."

When had she lost control of the situation and the conversation? Dani wondered frantically. She sat there and listened, still in shock, while the other four people in the room planned her future for her. They set a date barely a month away, they made plans for the wedding itself, the reception, and suggested some honeymoon spots. Nick went right along with all their plans.

"What do you intend to do about a dress, Dani?" her mother finally asked.

"Good question," she replied, giving Nick a level look.

"What about yours?" John asked his wife. "Dani's about the same size as you were when we married."

"Well," Sarah said, looking at Dani, "I'm not sure that she wouldn't want something a little more modern than mine."

"Nonsense," Nick said. "I bet Dani would look lovely in your gown. I've seen your wedding pictures. You looked gorgeous, Sarah."

Dani watched her mother blush with confusion. The truth was that her mother *had* looked wonderful in her wedding pictures. The dress had been beautiful with its full train covered with seed pearls. Dani, whenever she gave it a thought, had always assumed she would be married in her mother's wedding gown. After all, that was why her mother had saved it.

"Why don't we go upstairs now and have you try it on?" Sarah suggested. "That will give us some idea what alterations need to be done."

Dani involuntarily looked to Nick, hoping for help. She should have known better.

"What a great idea, darling," he said, patting Dani's hand. "I'm sure John and I can entertain ourselves down here while you women take care of the gown."

Dani wondered what he would do if she were to pick up the beautiful floral centerpiece on the table and brain him with it? He'd probably smile provocatively and call her "darling" a few dozen more times.

As soon as she got upstairs she turned to her mother. "I'm not sure what Nick is trying to do, Mom, but, you see—"

Sarah laughed and patted Dani's shoulder. "I should think it's obvious, Dani," she said archly. "The man has decided he's waited long enough for you. Now he's impatient to claim you."

Dani rolled her eyes. "He's really not serious, Mom. The only reason—"

"How can you say that? One look at the man would tell you he's very serious. Why, the loving way he looks at you almost brings tears to my eyes." She hugged Dani ferociously. "Do you have any idea how thankful I am to see the two of you finally together? My prayers have been answered." She opened the large storage closet in the spare bedroom and disappeared. Within minutes she came out carrying a large white box. As soon as she placed it on the bed, Sarah opened it.

Mona had followed them upstairs and was in time to see the lid being removed. "Oh, Sarah, how beautiful."

Dani's mother beamed. "I've always thought so. We'll have to have it cleaned, of course, but I think it's still in good shape." She began to pull the gown out of the box, fluffing it out. Dani stood there and allowed the two women to slip the gown over her head, mutter about the waistline, pin up the hem and in general flutter like a couple of butterflies around her, while she stood in the middle of the room, staring at herself in the large oval mirror on the wall.

Didn't Nick care what he was doing to his own mother, never mind *her* mother's feelings? Didn't he understand how hurt they were going to be when she and Nick told them that the wedding was off?

And what about the invitations? They were already making up lists, for God's sake. Did he want them to be totally embarrassed, not to mention all the pre-wedding expenses, when it became necessary to announce that they'd changed their minds?

Nick Montgomery had always been her knight in shining armor, her guardian angel. It had only taken one afternoon for him to fall off the pedestal where she'd placed him for most of her life. And boy, when he fell, did he ever make a splash.

She'd never seen the cruel insensitive side to the man, never guessed at the sadistic streak that ran through his nature.

Now that she had, she knew that she would never feel the same way about Nick again. She'd lost her hero—and it hurt.

Her eyes blurred as they filled with tears.

"You are going to be a beautiful bride, my dear," Mona said softly, touching Dani's hand. "Nick is a very lucky man. I was so afraid he would lose you before he woke up to the fact that he loved you so much."

Oh, Nick, how can you be so cruel? None of us deserves this. Are you paying me back for all the times I upset you when we were growing up?

Is this your idea of revenge because I caused your engagement to break up?

Dani blinked her eyes to clear them and stared at the calm young woman standing in the floating white dress, with the two older women kneeling as they pinned up the hem.

I never meant you any harm, Nick. You must have known that. I will never forgive you for what you are doing to me now.

Chapter Seven

"Dani? I'm going to need your help tonight," Frank said, walking over to where she sat working. "Would it be possible for you to stay for a while?"

Dani had been so engrossed in her own tasks that she jumped when he first spoke to her. "I think so. What do you need?"

He began to explain and Dani caught the air of suppressed excitement about him. He must have discovered something. She wondered why he wanted her to be around if he, in fact, had managed a breakthrough in their research. Whatever his reason, she was pleased that he had asked her.

When they finally stopped for the night it was after ten o'clock and they were both exhausted and hungry.

"Want to get something to eat before we go home?" Frank asked as they left the building, after signing out at the security guard's desk.

"Sounds good."

"I'll meet you at the corner diner on Elm Street," he said with a slight wave before heading toward his car.

Now that they were away from the lab Dani began to realize what she had done—or more to the point, not done. She hadn't called Nick, which she had promised to do each evening to let him know she was all right.

She didn't know why he was treating this situation like some spy thriller in which her life was being threatened. Although there was no doubt that Frank was falsifying formulas and information, Dani knew there was no danger to her.

One of the reasons she was so upset was that Frank had become a friend of hers, and even now she found herself looking for excuses for his behavior. Maybe he needed money, although she was the first to admit that they received excellent salaries and benefits at Merrimac.

If only he would talk to her about what was happening. She didn't dare bring up the subject. It would hinder the investigation, of which she knew she was a vital part. Betrayal was an interesting subject, one that Dani had never explored before. She knew that, regardless of the outcome, she would feel as though her choice had been to betray either Frank or the company for which they both were paid to work. She had already made her choice, but it didn't take away the pain of losing a friend.

As soon as they reached the small restaurant Dani excused herself and went to the pay phone just outside the rest rooms.

Nick answered on the first ring.

"Hi. It's me."

"Where the hell have you been, Dani? It's almost eleven o'clock."

"At work."

"Alone?"

Here it comes. "No. With Frank."

"Have you lost your mind?"

"Nick, what you need to understand is that Frank and I have been working together for more than a year now. He's the head of the research team and, as such, is the man I report to. When he asks me to work late I do it."

"Did you notify Worthington?"

"No. I saw no reason to notify him that we'd decided to work late. It's not that unusual."

"Where are you now?"

"At one of the local diners. We thought we'd get something to eat before going home."

"We? As in you and Frank?"

"That's right." She glanced at her watch. "Look, Nick, if it will make you feel any better I'll call you when I get home. Right now I'd like to go and eat. I'm hungry."

"I'm sorry, Dani. I wasn't thinking. I've just been so damned worried about you."

"I apologize for not calling you sooner. I'll talk to you later."

When she returned to the table the food had already been delivered. She smiled at Frank as she sat down across from him. "Sorry to be so long."

He took a bite of his food before answering. "You called your fiancé?"

She could feel herself blushing. "Yes." Hastily she picked up her hamburger and took a bite.

"It still seems strange to me knowing you're planning to get married. In all this time we've known each other, you never talked about a man in your life."

"I suppose there was never any reason to. You and I have generally discussed the progress of our work, or current events, or some social happening. We never got around to discussing personal matters."

He gave her a half smile. "I suppose I took it for granted that we would have time for all of that later."

She forced herself to meet his eyes. "We're friends, Frank. There was no reason for us to try to make our relationship into anything else."

"I know." He picked up his sandwich and began to eat in earnest.

By the time Dani pulled up in front of her apartment she ached with weariness. She fumbled with her purse as she neared the door, then let out a small scream when she saw movement in the shadows by her door.

"It's just me. Don't panic," Nick said.

"What are you doing here?"

He took the key from her hand and opened the door. "I would think that would be obvious." He turned on a lamp and moved through the apartment, checking each room.

She leaned against the closed front door and shook her head. "You're really getting into this whole thing, aren't you? As a matter of curiosity, just who are you looking for? Since I just left Frank, there's no way he could have beat me home—on the off chance he wanted to lurk in a closet or under the bed."

He reappeared from the back bedroom and strode down the hallway toward her.

"One of us needs to take this seriously."

"Oh, I'm serious about it. I just don't see any danger to me in all of this." She walked toward him. "Who are you looking for?"

"He has to have accomplices. He can't be doing this alone."

"On the contrary, I'm convinced that is exactly what he's doing. I just don't know why."

"Have you managed to get any more information?"

"Yes, but I'm not able to discuss it with you or anyone."

He studied her for a moment. "You look tired."

"Imagine that."

"Why don't you go take a hot bath?"

"That's exactly what I intend to do as soon as you go home."

"Don't mind me. I'll have something warm for you to drink when you come out."

She shook her head. She was too tired to argue.

As soon as she filled the tub with steamy water and scented bath crystals Dani eased her aching body into the water.

She was used to spending days hunched over her work. It was always a relief to get home and relax. She even recognized the added tension of monitoring Frank without his being aware of it.

No. Frank wasn't the problem. Or at least, the problem Frank posed was under control.

Nick was the problem in her life at the moment, one she didn't know how she was going to solve.

She didn't know what she was going to do about him. After their weekend in New Jersey she had contacted the agents and discussed the expected period of time before they confronted Frank. The news hadn't been encouraging.

Dani could understand how carefully they needed to gather their evidence. They had to have proof, not just her word. If they could discover his motive and what he hoped to accomplish, their task would be easier.

What irritated her was the fact that there had been no necessity for the bogus engagement. Frank had accepted that there was someone else in her life. The news article had taken their simple ruse and blown it into gigantic proportions. What upset her the most was that Nick didn't seem to care.

He was going along with their parents' plan as though the two of them would go through with a wedding. She had to talk to him about it but had wanted a few days to think about how she would approach him. Her first reaction had been anger, then pain at his cavalier attitude.

Perhaps tonight would be a good time to discuss how he intended to put a stop to the momentum that had begun with their visit home last weekend.

By the time she rejoined Nick in the tiny space that she called her kitchen, Dani had braced herself for a confrontation. She had put on her pajamas and robe, but left her feet bare. When she walked in he poured her a cup of hot chocolate.

"How many times over the years have you plied me with hot chocolate?" she murmured, taking the cup from him. He motioned for her to return to the living room, where he followed her with a cup of his own.

"It was always a guaranteed way to cheer you up."

"And you think I need cheering?"

"I'm not sure. All I know is that you've avoided me the entire week. I had made up my mind that I'd take you to dinner tonight and we'd get to the bottom of whatever is going on with you."

"I think you know me well enough to recognize what's wrong."

He nodded, taking a sip of chocolate. "You're upset about the wedding arrangements."

"Bingo."

He set down his cup and spread his hands. "All right. Let's look at all of this logically. You needed someone else in your life at the moment."

"That's already a debatable fact. Frank would not have given me a hard time about not seeing him outside of work. I realize that now. I just wish I hadn't panicked at first. I wasn't sure how I was going to act around him. And yet I've had no trouble with him. He's easy to work for and to work with."

"I think the whole problem here is you're in love with Frank."

She groaned. "Nick, I love you dearly but that writer's imagination of yours drives me crazy at times. And in case you're wondering, this is one of those times."

They were seated at opposite ends of the couch. He turned so that he was facing her. "Is that the truth?"

"Absolutely. You are driving me crazy."

"No! I don't mean that. You said that you love me dearly. Is that true?"

She stared at him as though he was the one claiming to be out of his mind. "Nick, you know very well that I have loved you for ages—I've bombarded you with my homemade valentines, sent you mushy birthday cards, and as for Christmas—"

"I know, I know. But that was all kid stuff."

"Since I was a child at the time, I find that most appropriate myself. What do you want from me?"

He ran his hand through his hair, then shook his head as though trying to clear it. "My God, I feel like a sophomore again."

She inched over until she was close enough to take his hand. "Nick," she said in a low soothing voice. "I still love you. Surely you know that. You have always been my hero, the brother I never had, my savior whenever I got myself into a mess I couldn't handle alone."

"A brother," he repeated in a monotone.

"Right. And my very best friend. You've always encouraged me. Even when you were upset with the way I went about things, you applauded the effort I made. You've helped me to slow down a little, not to be quite so impulsive—"

"Not so you would notice," he pointed out dryly.

"The thing is, I've always known you were there for me. That you were on my side. Until now."

He'd been looking away from her, but when she added the last two words his head whipped around. "What are you talking about?"

"You don't seem to care how much I'll be embarrassed when we call off the wedding. No matter how we do it, it will be obvious that Nick Montgomery chose not to marry the girl next door. Nobody's going to blame you, least of all me. After all, I know the engagement is a fake. But no one else does. And the way you're encouraging everybody, it's real to them. And those are the people I'm going to have to face."

"Then marry me," he said quietly.

"Nick!" She jumped up from the couch and began to pace. "That's not the answer and you know it. How can you even suggest such a thing?"

"What's wrong with the idea?"

She spun on her heel and glared at him. "To begin with, I don't want to get married at this stage in my life. And second, when I do decide to get married I want it to happen because the man I marry loves me, not because he needs to save me from another one of my scrapes."

"I love you, Dani."

She stopped and put her hands on her hips. "I know you do, Nick. You always have. But we're talking about a different kind of love here."

"Maybe you'd better explain the difference to me. I'm afraid I'm a little confused."

She nodded. "Of course you are, but I'm too tired to go into it with you at the moment. Believe me, one of these days I'll be attending your wedding and watching you walk out of the church with a tall redhead with a fantastic body on your arm!''

The clutch of pain that her word picture caused Dani surprised her. Of course Nick would get married some day. She had always known that. She had consoled herself with the notion that even if he did, he would still be there for her when she needed him. Dani had used that thought as a talisman to keep her from feeling devastated at the possible loss of Nick from her life.

''Dani?''

She hadn't noticed that he'd gotten to his feet and was standing in front of her. She tilted her head and looked up at him.

''I'm engaged to you,'' he pointed out softly.

''Temporarily.''

''We don't know how long this investigation is going to last.''

She sighed. ''I know that.''

''If we were married I would be able to stay with you at night to make sure you were all right. Have you ever thought of that?''

Dani thought of the number of nights she had lain awake thinking about the mess at work, wondering what Frank had gotten himself into and how it might affect her. She had even thought about the possibility that he might have cohorts who could harm her. But she wasn't going to share those thoughts with Nick.

"I'm a grown woman, Nick. I can take care of myself."

He sat beside her and put his arms around her. "Dani? Would you trust me to do what I think is best in this matter?"

"I'm not sure. You've been acting rather peculiar lately."

He grinned in response to her remark. "I really think we should go ahead with the wedding plans."

"Why?"

"There are lots of reasons. It's not as though we're a couple of strangers who know nothing about each other."

"We know too much about each other."

"Maybe."

"And we could end up hurting each other."

"I would never do anything to hurt you, Dani. You know that."

"Not intentionally, anyway."

"If you don't like it we could always have the marriage annulled or something."

"So what you're saying is that we get married but only pretend to live together?"

He looked the epitome of innocence. "Whatever you say. You can set whatever rules you want."

"I take it you would expect me to move in with you?"

"It's customary, but not mandatory."

"Just until this case is properly concluded."

"Your rules, remember?"

"How are you going to handle the fact that you might want to date someone else?"

"I'll try to control the urge, okay?" he replied with amusement and pulled her into his arms. Before she could say anything he leaned down and kissed her.

Darn it, why did he keep doing that to her? She couldn't think when he kissed her and right now she needed to think very badly. There was something she was missing here, something that didn't quite fit. Nick Montgomery wasn't the self-sacrificing sort. Why would he want to marry her?

The kiss finally claimed her full attention. When he stopped, her head was spinning.

"I wish you wouldn't do that," she muttered, closing her eyes once again.

"You don't like my kissing you?"

"I find it very distracting."

"You don't like my kissing you?" he repeated.

"I don't dislike it. I just would prefer that you didn't. Your kisses tend to muddle my thinking."

"Maybe your thinking needs muddling."

"I never thought I'd live to hear you say that!"

"No doubt I'm mellowing in my old age."

"Nick, I'm going to be in my old age if you don't go home and let me get some sleep. I don't know about you but I have to work in the morning. I can't sleep until noon—"

"Neither can I! Is that the sort of life you think I lead?"

"I don't know, Nick. That's my point. We've been out of touch for the last few years. I knew you as a child, as a teenager and through your college years. You're not the same person I grew up with."

"I'm not?"

"Well, of course you are in some respects. It's just that there's so much more that goes into making a relationship work than having grown up together."

He rubbed her cheek with his finger. "Don't worry about us, okay? Let the plans stay the way they are. If they manage to close the case before the proposed wedding date, we'll look at our options then. If not, we'll go on with the wedding."

"But don't you understand? If we called off the engagement now, it still served its purpose. Frank isn't going to insist on resuming our relationship."

"I'm making damned sure he won't."

"I don't understand this jealous act you keep putting on."

"Not jealous. Protective."

"Whatever you want to call it, I find it silly and unnecessary."

"If you'll marry me, I won't act jealous or protective again, I promise. I'll neglect you like a proper husband should."

She eyed him uncertainly. "Do you really think marriage is necessary?"

He nodded, looking very serious. Dani gazed at him for a long time in silence. This was Nick, whom she would trust with her life. He wasn't always predictable, but he could always be counted on when she needed him.

Perhaps she needed him now more than she wanted to admit. For whatever his reasons, he wanted her to marry him, even though it would not be a consummated marriage.

Finally she nodded. "All right, Nick. I'll marry you."

Chapter Eight

Once again Dani found herself staring at her image in a mirror. Once again she was wearing her mother's wedding gown. This time the dress fit as though it had been made for her, which in a way it had been. The waist had been taken in, the hem shortened, and the dress had been carefully cleaned and refurbished.

The sound of organ music played softly in the distance. Her mother peeked around the door and came inside the room where Dani continued to stare into the mirror.

"You look like a storybook princess, Dani," she said.

"Thank you."

"Why are you so sad?"

"I'm scared, Mom. Really scared. I can't quite figure out what I'm doing here, getting ready to marry Nick in a few moments."

Sarah smiled. "I understand the feeling perfectly. I felt exactly the same way the day I married your father."

Dani turned away from her image and looked at her mother. "You did?"

"Of course. I think every woman does, and from what I've heard, men have a similar reaction. The ritual of marriage brings home the commitment you are making, and commitments are always scary, no matter how long you've known the other person, or how much you love him."

"I do love Nick, Mom. I just don't think I should be marrying him. What if I can't make him happy?"

"Did he ask you to?"

"Of course not. It's just understood."

"I don't think so. What each of you has agreed on is to see to your own happiness within the framework of the commitment you're making to each other."

"I don't think I'm ready for marriage."

"You must be, or you wouldn't be standing here now."

"That's why I'm so confused. What am I doing here?"

Sarah laughed. "Believe me, once you start down that aisle and see Nick waiting for you, you'll remember why you agreed to marry him."

Strangely enough her mother was right. Her father escorted her from the small room where she had dressed, then they began the cadenced walk down the middle of the small church that she and Nick had attended for years.

Never had she seen him look so handsome. He wore a powder-blue tuxedo that matched the color of his eyes, the same eyes that watched intently as she slowly moved toward him. He didn't smile, but there was a sparkle in his eyes that caused the heat to rise in her cheeks.

The ceremony itself became a blur in her mind and later Dani could recall only flashes of it: the sound of Nick's deep voice repeating the vows in a strong firm tone; the smell of the scented candles and the flowers in the bouquet her mother had ordered for her; the sight of the slight tremor in Nick's fingers as he slipped the wedding ring on her finger; the touch of his lips pressed briefly against hers; the sound of the organ music as it swelled into a triumphant march as they turned and faced their friends and family. She remembered seeing the tears on their mothers' faces, hearing Nick's amused laugh and the tug she felt in her chest when several of her college friends made a production out of kissing the groom while the bride received her best wishes.

The reception hall was filled with voices chattering and laughing. She and Nick went through the ceremony of cutting the cake for the benefit of the photographer. A small band played and she and Nick led the dancing. All of it seemed unreal, and Dani allowed herself to float along in the dreamlike atmosphere.

By the time they managed to get away it was already dark.

She was still wearing her wedding gown and Nick made a laughing production out of getting her and the dress in his small sports car.

When he got in beside her she asked, "Where are we going?"

He was quiet for a moment as he started the car and drove away from the waving friends and family.

"After much thought I decided to take you back to my place. I think we'd both be more comfortable there than pulling up in front of a hotel dressed like this." He glanced down at his formal attire.

Dani recognized her feeling to be one of relief. She enjoyed Nick's home. It was rambling and comfortable. They had moved her things over there from her apartment two days before, and she had turned in her key to the superintendent when Nick came by to pick her up the day before. They had spent the previous night with their parents.

They had done it. She and Nick were married. She still had trouble believing that they had actually gone through with the wedding. Nick's behavior was so out of character for him. Why he would choose to sacrifice himself in order to help her out, she would never know. But he had and she had accepted.

She had given Frank an invitation, and he'd sent her a gift but told her that he needed to work. Since she knew what he was working on, not only the sensitivity of it but the need for continual surveillance, she had understood. They couldn't both be gone.

Dani made sure that Mr. Worthington had been kept fully informed of each step of their research, that he was given each new piece of data as they discovered it and before Frank made his minute changes.

"Are you tired?" Nick asked after several miles of silence.

"A little. How about you?"

"Actually I enjoyed it. It was fun to see all our old friends and classmates again. I was surprised at the number of people who showed up."

"I think between your mother and mine they managed to keep up with every move made by families in the neighborhood."

"Sometimes we need to go back to our roots, I guess, to remind ourselves of who we are and what we've become."

"You should be pleased with who you've become—the famous playwright."

"I enjoyed being remembered today for other things."

She smiled, recalling some of the ribbing he'd taken today. "I wonder why no one seemed particularly surprised that we'd decided to get married."

He glanced at her. "All of my friends knew years ago that I'd never be able to get you out of my life."

She poked him in the arm. "Thanks a lot."

He rubbed his arm and groaned. "For such a little person, you can certainly pack a mean wallop."

"You deserved it. Get me out of your life indeed."

"Well, you have to admit that you certainly knew how to be a pest when you set out to be."

"I never tried to be a pest, I'll have you know. It just came naturally." Her outraged rejoinder was spoiled by a giggle.

He glanced at her again, then returned his eyes to the road. "We're going to do just fine, Dani. We won't rush anything—just take one day at a time. Once the situation at your work gets straightened out, we'll decide where we want to go from there, okay?"

She nodded. "It's too late for regrets now, wouldn't you say?"

"How can you suggest such a possibility? We're both going to be deliriously happy. I'll write the best plays that have ever been seen, you'll discover a new way of cleaning the impurities from your silicon wafers, and we'll both retire at the tops of our fields."

They spent the drive back to Connecticut talking about the wedding and reception, about the people who had come, about the food, about every possible subject—except the coming night, their first night together as a married couple.

As soon as they pulled into the driveway and stopped, Nick turned and looked at Dani. "We're home."

She played with a fold of her satin gown. "So we are."

He opened his door, got out and walked around to the other side. When he opened the door he said, "Are you in there under all that material?"

If she didn't know him so well she probably wouldn't have heard the strain in his voice. He wasn't as relaxed as he was pretending to be, Dani realized, with a feeling of relief.

She held out her hand and he tugged, helping her to her feet. Before she realized his intentions he swept her up in his arms. "See, I've already practiced this one. And I have the key in my hand."

After unlocking the door he carried her across the threshold and stopped. Balloons and streamers decorated the foyer and a giant sign that spelled *congratulations* hung across the archway into the front room.

"It looks as though Dorothy, my house-keeper, has been busy." He slowly lowered her to her feet. "Uh, do you want to change clothes?"

"I'd love to. Unfortunately I can't get out of this thing on my own. There must be a hundred buttons fastening the back."

He took her hand and led her down the hall-way to his bedroom. She had never been to the back part of the house before. This part was his private domain—his bedroom, bath and the of-fice where he wrote.

She assumed that she would sleep upstairs, where she had on the other occasion she had been there.

He opened the door and continued to lead her so that she had no choice but to follow him into a large room with windows on three sides. In the daylight nature's scenic beauty must have contributed an ever changing array of colors to be enjoyed by the room's occupant.

A massive stone fireplace took up a large portion of one wall, but it was the bed that drew her attention. Situated on a dais, the bed looked large enough to sleep six or more people comfortably.

He let go of her hand and turned her around. Humming to himself, Nick set about undoing her dress.

"This is a beautiful room, Nick.'

"Thanks. I enjoy it."

"It's very peaceful."

"Mmmhmm."

"You probably don't hear anything from the rest of the house."

"I planned it that way."

"You mean you built this house? I thought you just found it and bought it."

"Nope," he said absently, still unbuttoning. "I explained to an architect what I wanted and he drew it up for me."

The top of her dress began to fall away from her shoulders and she grabbed it, pressing it against her chest.

"There you go. All done."

She glanced over her shoulder nervously. "I feel so silly. I should have remembered to lay out something to put on first."

He walked over to a door and opened it, exposing a walk-in closet the size of the bedroom in her old apartment. He reappeared, carrying her robe. "Is this okay?"

Her eyes widened. "What's this doing in here?"

He looked surprised. "Where did you expect it to be?"

"Well, I, uh, hadn't really given it much thought. I mean, I suppose I was thinking I'd use the same bedroom as before."

"Don't be silly. There's no reason we can't share." He waved his hand. "Obviously there's plenty of room."

"Oh. Well, I suppose it would make sense."

"I'll see what Dorothy left in the fridge for us to eat. Come on out when you get changed."

"I'll do that," Dani muttered faintly as he strode out of the bedroom. Out of *their* bedroom. Why hadn't it occurred to her that he would expect her to share his room? They'd talked about the marriage being temporary, hadn't they? Surely she remembered his saying something to that effect. Why had she assumed that temporary meant separate quarters?

She pulled her arms out of the long sleeves of the gown and stepped out of the garment. The dress practically stood on its own. She crossed the room and opened a door that she assumed led into the bathroom. She'd been right, but was not prepared for the luxury she found. The glass-enclosed shower was large enough for several people, and the Jacuzzi had steps leading up to it. The mirrored walls reflected ferns and other greenery.

Dani had no idea this part of Nick's personality existed. She finished undressing and stepped into the shower, enjoying the soothing spray on her overheated skin.

As soon as she was through, she dried herself with one of the softest, deepest-pile towels she'd ever seen. Then she went in search of her clothes.

Underwear had been tucked away in a chest of drawers; slacks and a blouse were in the closet. She found slippers and, after taking a final look at herself, decided she was ready to rejoin Nick.

She found him at the dining-room table setting out various dishes filled with tempting foods. He'd removed his jacket and tie, and rolled the sleeves of his frilly shirt a couple of times up his forearms.

He glanced up when she walked in. "Feeling better?"

Suddenly Dani felt shy with her childhood friend. "Much better, thank you."

"Why don't you start filling a plate with what you want while I go change? I won't be but a moment."

"I'm sorry. I didn't mean to take so long."

"No problem."

She watched as he walked out of the room. Why did she feel as though she'd gone into some strange time warp where everything looked the same but in fact was very different? Nick was no longer Nick, her friend. He was now Nick, her husband. This was no longer a house that she visited on occasion. It was her home, the only one she had.

She finished filling her plate and sat down. Nick came back in and she almost groaned aloud. He had looked great in the formal clothes, but there was something about the way his faded jeans clung to his legs that strongly affected her. The knit shirt he'd pulled over his head had messed up his hair and now clung to his torso like a second skin. He brushed his fingers through the tousled hair that lay across his forehead.

"Good, you're eating."

"Actually I was waiting for you."

"Don't do that. I'll catch up." He busied himself with a plate, then sat across from her.

Why was she suddenly so nervous? She felt like
a silly schoolgirl, not a grown woman. She was
acting as though this man was a stranger, not the
guy who used to hold her hand to cross the street
when she was a little girl.

"What do you think?"

She glanced up, startled. "About what?"

He gestured to the table. "The food, everything. Do you like it? Is there some favorite dish
you want that you could tell Dorothy about? I
think she's a pretty good cook but if you—"

"Oh, I think she's a wonderful cook, really
great. I'm afraid I don't do that much cooking
really. So anything is fine." She stopped and laid
her fork on her plate. "Nick, I don't want to
change your routine or anything while I'm here.
I just want you to go on with your life as though
I didn't exist."

"That might be a little hard to do, you know."

"At least I'll be gone during the day when
you're writing. So I won't disturb you there."

"By the way, I almost forgot. We've been invited to a round of parties next week in Manhattan. I'm afraid I couldn't say no. Everyone wants
to meet you. The cast is throwing a special event
in your honor. I know how you hate those things,
but I couldn't think of a way to get out of them."

"Oh, Nick. I don't know how much I will be
able to get away right now. We're really coming

close to a new breakthrough and it might mean some long hours. Couldn't you go without me?"

He studied her for a moment in silence, then looked away. "I suppose so."

Dani had never seen that particular expression on Nick's face before. He didn't look angry exactly. Hurt, perhaps? She heard herself say, "I'll try to get time off. We'll just have to see how it goes."

He looked down at his place. "Sure. I understand."

Dani felt a sudden need to explain. "It isn't as if all of this is real. I mean, we don't have to pretend to be madly in love, do we?"

He didn't look at her. Instead he picked up his glass and said, "I suppose everyone thinks that's the reason we decided to marry. Because we were madly in love."

She flushed at her own obtuseness. "Oh, of course. That was the whole point of the engagement."

"It doesn't matter."

She reached out and touched his hand. "I'll see about getting off. Just tell me which days, okay?"

Dani had a difficult time finishing her dinner but she doggedly ate until she'd cleaned her plate. She didn't know why the lump had formed in her throat. Perhaps it was because Nick had become so quiet, speaking only in response to her occasional question.

She hadn't meant to hurt him but she knew she had somehow. She was always so wrapped up in her work and in the situation there that she hadn't given much thought to how all the publicity had affected him.

They put the food away in silence. Then Dani excused herself and returned to the bedroom. She found her nightgown and slipped it over her head, crawled into the side of the bed opposite the clock radio and reading lamp, assuming that was the side Nick generally slept on, and turned off the bedside lamp. The bathroom light cast a glow into the room.

She lay in bed for a long time, wondering when Nick might be coming to bed, but the events of the day gradually overtook her and she fell asleep.

It was past midnight before Nick entered the bedroom. From the open doorway he could see Dani's tousled curls, their inky blackness vivid against the bright hue of the pillow case. She had the covers pulled high around her neck, only the tip of her nose and the crown of her head visible.

Why had he told Dorothy to move Dani's things into his room? He must have been crazy.

He'd had great plans for tonight. He knew that Dani loved him. He knew that he loved her. Tonight he'd planned to tell her just how much, and how much he wanted this marriage to be permanent.

When had it hit him how much she meant to him? When he'd realized that she could be in danger? When he saw the look on his face in the picture of them at the restaurant? When had he discovered that Dani wasn't the pest, the bane of his existence, the nemesis of his childhood?

He couldn't point out the exact instant in time. He just knew that it was so.

And now he knew that she thought of him like a brother. A brother, for God's sake!

He had fully intended to show her the difference between loving a brother and loving a husband tonight, had determined that by the next morning Dani Devereaux Montgomery would feel truly married and loved by her husband.

Only to discover that he couldn't do it. He couldn't take advantage of the situation that way. He loved her, yes. But he didn't want her to feel trapped. From the way she responded to his kisses he had allowed himself to hope that she would respond to him more fully now that they were married.

But he was a coward. He was afraid to take a chance on her rejecting him. So now she was asleep in his bed on their wedding night. And what did he intend to do about it?

Nothing. Not a thing.

He shook his head, calling himself all kinds of a fool. If he'd written this kind of a scenario in one of his plays, no one would have believed it. He was in love with his wife and didn't know how to deal with his feelings.

He'd told her how he felt, but she hadn't understood, and he wasn't sure how to make her understand because it was obvious that she didn't feel the same way.

He would have to listen to his own advice: take each day as it came. He wouldn't put any pressure on her, but would allow her to get used to living with him. They would set up a routine, enjoy each other's company and wait for something to break at Merrimac.

That would have to be enough for now. All he had to do was sleep next to her night after night, share a bathroom, closet, bedroom and bed with her so that he would be constantly reminded of her light floral scent, the sound of her soft sighs when she slept or her off-key humming when she was in the shower, watch her padding around in her underwear and treating him like a pet poodle.

Nick had never before noticed these masochistic tendencies in his personality. It was too late now to do anything about them.

Chapter Nine

Dani smiled brightly at the group of people surrounding her. It was the third party she and Nick had attended in the past two weeks. Occasionally sipping from her champagne glass, Dani concentrated on appearing composed and friendly. Not by a flicker of an eyelash or the slightest tightening of her mouth did she betray her thoughts about the tall redheaded woman who was at that very moment standing beside Nick, who was across the room from Dani. The woman was seductively stroking his arm while she hung on to every word he uttered.

Dani wondered what the woman would look like with a faceful of champagne? It would be a humane thing for Dani to do, she decided judiciously, because the woman obviously needed cooling off.

In her current mood, Dani felt that she was just the person to be able to help the redhead.

Tonight wasn't the cause of her mood and she knew it. Neither was the woman. However, the woman was a very visible symptom of what was getting to Dani: her relationship with Nick.

Or to be more precise, her lack of a relationship with Nick. They had been closer, more friendly toward each other during the coldest of the cold wars they'd waged during their growing-up years than they had been during the past two weeks.

How could that possibly be? They were adults now, and married. Most important of all, they were married *to each other!*

So why had she become invisible to Nick since their wedding? He didn't ignore her. He was always polite to her. He just didn't *see* her.

And his attitude was driving her crazy. *He* was driving her crazy.

Her thoughts returned, as they seemed to do with dismaying frequency, to their wedding night. She had fallen asleep before Nick came to bed that night. Some time during the night she awakened, disoriented. Moonlight streamed through one of the many windows in the room and she propped herself up on her elbow and looked around.

The first thing she saw was Nick, sprawled on the other side of the bed, his head half-buried under his pillow. The sheet he had used for a cover had been kicked aside and was wrapped around part of one leg. Her gaze skimmed the long expanse of his tanned back down to the paler expanse of flesh that obviously rarely saw the light of day.

He'd come to bed nude.

Dani blinked in astonishment, then felt waves of heat flow over her. Since his head was turned away from her, she could only see the nape of his neck. Thank God he wasn't awake to see her reaction to him.

It wasn't as though she'd never seen his body before, or most of it, anyway. But it was amazing what a shock it was to find those few inches of bare flesh uncovered after all these years. She felt like a fool, overreacting to such an extent, and could only be glad that he slept on his stomach. If she'd rolled over and found him lying there on his back with no—

She wouldn't think about it. She was being ridiculous. There was nothing to be afraid of, after all. Nick wasn't about to attack her. Hadn't he said something about her making the rules? Perhaps she should have paid more attention to that detail. Somehow she didn't see Nick being willing to agree to sleep in pajamas in order not to shock her modesty.

Dani eased back onto her pillow and lay there, staring up at the ceiling. This was not what she had imagined her wedding night to be. If she was honest with herself, she had never given weddings, marriages and wedding nights much thought over the years. Her goal had been focused on a career. Men and marriage were hazy thoughts for later.

Besides, she'd always known she could turn to Nick whenever she needed masculine advice or assistance. There had been no need to consider anyone else in her life.

She glanced over at him and realized that, if she chose to do so, she could reach out and touch his arm, which lay stretched out toward her. His fingers were curled slightly as though waiting for her. She could slip her hand inside that curl and feel safe.

Dani had always felt safe with Nick, hadn't she? So why was her heart fluttering in her chest and her breathing so shaky?

She finally managed to fall asleep again but her dreams were all confused. Nick kept appearing, then disappearing, and she felt as though she was wandering around in some sort of maze, trying to find her way out with no help from anyone.

The next time she woke bright sunlight poured through the windows and Nick stood beside the bed with a cup of coffee. She was immediately aware that this time he had on another pair of his well-worn jeans. She harbored no curiosity about what was concealed beneath them. Not any more. She knew.

"I thought you might like some coffee," he said as soon as she opened her eyes.

She blinked a couple of times, then managed to push herself up into a sitting position. He handed her the cup.

"It looks like a gorgeous day. Can you think of anything you'd like to do today?"

What a time for her to blush! But she could feel the heat sweep over her.

She shook her head without looking up at him.

He stretched across the end of the bed in a lounging position and propped himself up on one elbow. "How'd you sleep?"

"Fine." She still wouldn't look at him.

He laughed. "I woke up this morning and had the shock of my life to find someone in bed with me." His eyes danced. "I forgot you were here."

"I guess it'll take a little getting used to for both of us."

"Yeah, that's what I was thinking." He watched her for several moments in silence. "I guess we'll need to work out some sort of morning routine, like who showers first, that sort of thing."

"I guess so."

He rolled over so that he was lying on his back. Without any prompting her gaze slid the length of him, from the top of his blond head, down his bare chest, over his snug jeans, down to his bare toes. Then slowly she reversed the action.

"How do you keep your body so trim?" she heard herself ask with something akin to horror that she had spoken her thoughts aloud.

He'd closed his eyes but at her question they opened in surprise. "I chop a lot of wood, do some jogging, lift weights every once in a while. Whenever I'm stuck for an idea, I find that physical exertion helps to clear my mind."

Even now, standing in the midst of a party, Dani could remember her embarrassment at the speculative look he'd given her.

Now he seemed totally engrossed in the woman who had claimed his attention.

Probably these past two weeks hadn't affected him at all, but they had destroyed Dani's concentration and peace of mind. Nick didn't seem to have any modesty where she was concerned. He would come out of the bathroom after his shower partially wrapped with an indecently small towel, find his briefs in a drawer and nonchalantly drop the towel before pulling the briefs on.

In addition, he didn't seem concerned with her own attempts at modesty. She'd been taking a shower one morning when he came into the bathroom looking for something. He'd offered an absent apology, found whatever it was he'd come in search of and walked out. The glass walls hadn't even had the courtesy of fogging up, which had left her feeling totally exposed to his view.

He didn't act as though he'd noticed.

Whenever they attended these parties he made certain that she was introduced to everyone before he drifted away to talk business or whatever.

At the moment the only business that redhead looked to be in the mood to discuss was personal business.

"Excuse me for a moment," Dani said suddenly to the man who was speaking to her. "I'll be right back."

Enough was enough. She had played the role of the tolerant mate as long as she could.

She marched over to where Nick stood, the redhead still sliding her hand along his shoulder and down his arm. As soon as Nick saw her he smiled his warm friendly smile and held out his arm to her. She immediately stepped into the curve he presented and laid her head on his chest.

"Lorraine, I don't think you've met my wife, Dani. Honey, this is Lorraine Draper. You've probably seen her on Broadway. She's quite an accomplished actress."

Dani felt a fleeting pleasure at the look of frustration that settled on Lorraine's face. Dani smiled and held out her hand. "I'm pleased to meet you, Ms. Draper."

The other woman reluctantly took the end of Dani's fingers and immediately dropped them.

"We were just talking about a play that opened last week off Broadway. Lorraine tells me it's exceptionally well done. I'll have to see about getting tickets for us," he said.

Dani thought of several rejoinders to that remark having to do with the body language Lorraine had been expressing, but decided that discretion was a virtue to be practiced and perfected. She knew she had a long way to go.

Dani smiled without saying anything.

Nick looked down at her. "Are you tired, darling? Are you ready to go home?"

The suggestion sounded heavenly, but she knew she wasn't being fair. She'd been ready to leave as soon as they'd arrived.

"Whatever you want to do, Nick, is fine with me."

"Ah," Lorraine purred, "the perfect little wife. I thought adoring submissive wives were an extinct species."

Before Dani could say a word Nick laughed. "You must have Dani confused with someone else. She's as independent as they come. She's an engineer, by the way. And from all that I know about what she does, she's an excellent one."

Dani heard the pride in his voice with a feeling of surprise. They had not discussed her job much for the simple reason that most of it was classified. But somehow he knew how important it was to her. That pleased her.

He had apologized earlier for the round of parties, explaining that the invitations had come as a direct result of his most recent hit. He couldn't afford to ignore them at the moment, although most of the time he was able to send his regrets without a second thought.

He had assured her that this wasn't an example of what their life would be like. She'd found his explanation a little strange, since neither one of them had discussed the possibility of a future together. Hadn't they agreed that their marriage was serving a temporary purpose?

"I, for one, am ready to hit the road. We have a long drive ahead of us," Nick said.

"Oh, you mean you aren't staying in town overnight? Why not?" Lorraine asked.

Nick glanced down at Dani. "I don't know. I suppose we could, since you don't have to work tomorrow." He paused. "Or do you?"

"I'd planned to go in tomorrow afternoon. That shouldn't make a difference if you want to stay tonight."

The smile he gave her was almost devilish. "Then let's stay."

Lorraine smiled. "Good. Then there's no reason for you to rush off, is there?"

Nick's eyes never left Dani's. The gleam in them seemed to intensify as he said softly, "Oh, I don't know. I can think of one or two reasons myself."

Without looking at Lorraine he turned Dani toward the door and, leaning down, he whispered in her ear, "Let's tell our host good night, shall we?"

Dani hadn't seen Nick in this kind of mood before. She wasn't sure how to respond. The way he kept looking at her made her heart pound like a steam engine going up a steep grade.

They said all the polite things to their host, went downstairs and hailed a cab, and before long arrived at the Plaza.

Nick grinned as he took her hand and led her up the front steps of the hotel. "You do realize that no one is going to believe we're married. We don't have any luggage and you don't look old enough to be out at night without a sitter."

She glanced down at the dress she wore. "I hardly think a child would be wearing a dress like this."

He studied her carefully as they crossed the lobby to the desk. "That's true. A child would never be able to keep that top up." He laughed when she self-consciously placed her hand at the neckline of her gown.

He registered them with aplomb, explained that they would need a few things sent up to their room, such as toothbrushes and toothpaste. As soon as he was handed the key, he took her arm and started toward the bank of elevators. In a clear voice he asked, "What did you say your name was again, honey?"

Oh, he was going to pay for his warped sense of humor somehow, she would see to that.

He was still teasing her when they arrived at the door to their room and went inside. The first thing Dani noticed was the size of the bed. It was a double bed, but at first glance she would have said it would barely hold one person. Why hadn't she thought to suggest twin beds, or at the very least, a king-size one?

Nick didn't appear to notice. He began to loosen his tie and shed his coat. He sat down on the edge of the bed and slipped off his shoes. "What a good idea Lorraine had. I'm glad she mentioned it."

"Lorraine seemed to have a great many ideas tonight. How many of them were you encouraging?"

He stood and began to unbutton his shirt. "What are you talking about?"

"The way she was pawing you made me think of an oversexed alley cat."

"Really? I suppose you've been exposed to so many oversexed alley cats that you can immediately spot one in action?"

"No, but they're easy to identify."

He paused in unbuckling his pants and stared at her. "You're serious, aren't you? You're really upset about the way she was behaving."

"Of course not. I couldn't care less how she acted toward you."

"You wouldn't by any chance be jealous, would you?"

She had turned away and was taking off her jewelry but at his words she turned around in surprise. "Jealous? Me? Don't be silly."

He stepped out of his trousers and carefully folded them across the back of one of the chairs. Clad in only his briefs, Nick walked over to her and slipped his arms around her. He leaned over and began to nibble on her ear at the same time he began to unzip the back of her dress. "Maybe just a tiny bit?"

Chills ran across the expanse of flesh that his fingers and breath touched. "Of course not," she managed to say in a weak voice.

"You have no reason to be, you know," he whispered, placing featherlike kisses along her jaw to her chin and finally on her mouth.

"Mmm," he said after a moment. "You taste good." He kissed the base of her throat and behind her ears. "And you smell yummy." He nipped at her bare shoulder. "And I could eat you up, just like the Big Bad Wolf."

He laughed when she shivered, and picked her up, swinging around so that she grabbed him by the shoulders. Somehow her dress fell to the floor in that maneuver, leaving her in nothing more than a very tiny pair of panties, her garter belt, and her hose and shoes. Gently he placed her on the bed and with an expertise no doubt gained by a great deal of practice he slipped off her shoes, unsnapped her hose from their fastenings and slid them down her legs.

"Nick," she said breathlessly, "What are you doing?"

"Just helping you get ready for bed," he responded in his most innocent tone of voice.

He placed one knee on the bed and leaned over, turning out the light. He scooped the covers back and slid her under them, then crawled in beside her. There was enough light coming in the windows for her to see him, although his expression was hidden.

Nick stretched out beside her, placing his arm beneath her head and pulling her next to his body so that her head rested on his chest. "Aaah, it feels good to relax, doesn't it?"

How would she know? Dani was convinced that every muscle in her body had just gone into spasm.

"Are you comfortable?"

There was no way she could force a sound out of her paralyzed throat, so she nodded vigorously.

"Ever stayed at the Plaza before?" he asked conversationally.

She shook her head.

"I always try to stay here whenever possible."

Dani cleared her throat, hoping to remove the knot that seemed to have formed there.

"Are you going to be warm enough without your nightgown?" he asked solicitously.

Warm enough? Plastered against his hot body? Surely he jested. Dani felt as though her skin had already taken on scorch marks everywhere she touched him. And she was touching quite a lot of him at the moment. Did he really

think that she was going to be able to go to sleep
like that?

He took a deep breath and sighed, much like
Muffin returning home to sleep after a hard night
out on the town.

Dani started counting silently to herself, wondering how long she needed to lie there until it
would be safe for her to move. No doubt he
would be asleep in a very short while, which
would give her an opportunity to inch away from
him.

He shifted, running his hand along her spine;
with the other one, he tilted her head up to his.

His kiss was one of the most gentle she had
ever known. It was almost a benediction. Dani
found herself slowly beginning to relax under the
tender pressure of his lips.

When he shifted again, this time turning more
fully toward her, she scarcely noticed the slight
change in the intensity of the kiss, so caught up
was she in what she was feeling.

A sense of wonderment seemed to steal
through her, a sense of rightness. She returned
the pressure of his mouth, unconsciously pressing closer to him.

He eased his leg between hers and she obligingly tightened her thighs around it. Once again
he'd managed to turn her bones to mush, her
whole body feeling a liquid heat pour through it.

His hands never seemed to be still. They were busy touching, stroking, exploring, until all her senses were signaling Red Alert! Red Alert! All systems go!

The last scraps of clothing seemed to disappear from between them so that she was aware of every part of his body pressed snugly against hers.

She wanted him to put out the fires that he seemed to have started within her, but she didn't know how to tell him. She moaned, trying to get closer to him, needing him to show her what she must do to take care of the fever that suddenly seemed to grip her body.

Somehow he must have understood because he finally found the center of her need, filling her, completing her, carrying her off to a whole new realm of sensation that she had never known existed.

Dani clung to him, following his wordless instructions, responding in the most primitive way, trying to experience myriad feelings in a few moments of time.

How could she have been so unaware of such a marvelous part of life? Why hadn't Nick shown her such beauty of expression before now? How could he have allowed her to be deprived for so long?

Dani could only cling to him, thankful that he had at last shared with her the wonders of love-making, the joy of expressing herself in such an elemental way.

The groan that escaped him echoed her own. Dani felt as though she'd just left Earth's gravity and that she had been hurtled into space, with only Nick to guide her back.

Nick was all she needed to feel safe. He always had been. He always would be.

Nick. The man she loved. The man she would always love. The man who had agreed only to be her temporary husband had finally opened her eyes to a whole new world.

Nothing in her life would ever be the same again.

Chapter Ten

Nick stood in the shower, his arms braced against the wall, and let the hard spray of water rush over his head and body. The morning light had been accompanied by a harsh dose of reality and he was having difficulty accepting his behavior of the night before.

He had ignored his conscience and made love to Dani. He wasn't proud of himself. He could rationalize his actions by pointing out that he hadn't forced her and that she could have stopped him at any time. She had made her own choices.

Somehow his rational self wouldn't buy that explanation. Nick knew what he had done. He had seduced her, giving her little to no time to think about what was happening, little to no time to remind him of their agreement.

Damn their agreement. He loved her. He had married her because he loved her. And he wanted to make love to her. What was so bad about that?

She readily admitted that she loved him—and that was when his conscience kicked in. She loved him all right—like a brother, a friend, someone to turn to. And he had taken advantage of her trust in him out of a combination of frustration and fear of losing her.

Even now, he knew that given the same set of circumstances he would act in an identical manner. So much for having a conscience. It didn't make you behave any better. It just kept you from enjoying what you were determined to do anyway!

Yet another lie. Because he had thoroughly enjoyed loving her, experiencing her in the most physical way possible.

When he'd come awake earlier that morning she was still in his arms, her head nestled under his chin, her arm and leg lying across his body. So trusting. She had always trusted him, looked up to him, allowed him to take the lead. He'd certainly done that, hadn't he?

Nick finally reached over and turned off the water.

The question was, what did he do now? If he did what he wanted he would immediately return to that bed and spend the entire day making love to her. Obviously he hadn't learned a thing from the experience. He wasn't sure how he was going to look her in the eye and explain his behavior.

He would just have to play it by ear.

Dani stretched, then flinched. Her head was pounding, a sure sign that she shouldn't have had that second glass of champagne last night. Her body was protesting in some of the strangest places.

Then her eyes flew open as she remembered where she was and why she was tender in certain parts of her body. She was alone. She sat up, only then realizing that she had nothing on. Dani clutched the sheet to her chest and looked around.

Her dress still lay where she had stepped out of it the night before. Nick's jacket was tossed over one chair, his pants neatly folded across another. The steady sound of water falling from nearby finally impinged on her consciousness. Since the sun was shining, the noise must be coming from the bathroom.

At least that explained where Nick was.

Nick. The thought of him made her shiver as memories jostled each other in her mind, waiting to be recalled. Nick, looking so handsome in his formal wear. Nick, pulling her to him at the party, bragging about her abilities. Nick, peeling away her clothes and leaving her bare and vulnerable. Nick, kissing her, touching her, exploring and possessing her.

Nick.

She rolled over and hid her head under her pillow. What had happened to their comfortable and secure friendship? Where was her safe little world, her orderly existence? Where had all those ungovernable emotions that had swept over her the previous night come from?

And how was she going to face Nick again?

It wasn't that she was stupid or even particularly naive. What she was was inexperienced, although after last night she couldn't in all honesty admit to that, either.

Nick had taught her so much about herself and about life as they had grown up. Last night was the most explosive lesson she'd ever learned.

But what did it all mean? And where did they go from here?

She heard the water stop. He would be coming out soon and she didn't have a clue as to how to behave toward him now. She would just have to wing it and take her cue from him.

When the bathroom door opened Dani slowly raised her head and looked at him.

Her heart turned over in her chest. Once again he had somehow managed to find a less-than-adequate-size towel to wrap around his hips. She smiled. "Good morning."

He paused, glancing around the room before meeting her gaze. "Morning." His eyes darted away from hers. "I guess we'll have to put on last night's clothes, won't we?"

She grinned. "Either that, or we could mimic the television commercial and step out of the elevator wearing bath towels." Glancing down at the small towel that didn't quite meet across his thigh, she said, "But I think you might need to find a larger one, don't you?"

Nick realized that he'd been holding his breath. At least she wasn't angry, thank God. He released a quick sigh.

He sat down on the side of the bed and took her hand. "How are you feeling this morning?"

"Slightly hung over. I don't know why I drink champagne when it always gives me a headache."

Their eyes met for a brief moment, then each glanced away.

He opened his hand and looked at hers lying in his palm. She was so tiny. He followed the length of each of her fingers with one of his, as though tracing it, memorizing it, or as though he was trying to discover something about her from his intent regard.

"I, uh, I mean, we probably..." He paused and forced himself to glance up at her again. "We need to talk about last night, Dani."

His words, together with his grave expression, caused Dani's heart to sink. She pulled her hand from his grasp and hid it beneath the covers. Lifting her chin slightly, she replied, "If you say so."

Her attitude and tone weren't very encouraging, Nick decided, but they couldn't just ignore what had happened. How could they pretend it hadn't? Nick knew that he would never forget last night. Making love to Dani had been one of the most profound experiences of his life. If any doubt lingered in his mind about his feelings for her, last night had certainly erased them.

But that wasn't what upset him. He had broken their agreement. Although they hadn't specifically stated that they wouldn't make love, the implication had always been there.

So what could he say to her?

"I love you, Dani."

She slowly pushed herself up in bed. Why was he acting like this if he loved her? At the moment he was behaving the way he had when he was twelve and his pet mouse had died!

Obviously he was upset, but she didn't know what to do or say to let him know it was all right. She forced a smile on her face. "I know you do, Nick."

"You do?"

She nodded. "And I love you, too. So what's the problem with that? Are you sorry about last night?"

"Of course I am." Agitated, he came to his feet, almost losing his towel in the process. He found his briefs lying beside the bed and pulled them on without looking at her.

"I see," she said quietly.

"Making love to each other wasn't part of the deal."

Dani's heart sank. "No," she said slowly, "I don't suppose it was." She watched him step into his trousers and zip them up, then reach for his shirt.

Nick heard her agreement with dread. Why couldn't she argue with him? Why couldn't she tell him that their agreement no longer mattered because they loved each other?

The problem was that they had always loved each other in one way or the other. They were friends, for God's sake.

And he had betrayed the friendship.

"I want you to know that it won't happen again," he finally said, his eyes on the buttons of his shirt.

Dani felt as though he had hit her in the stomach with a fist. Without another word she crawled out of bed and, ignoring her nudity, walked the necessary few steps to the bathroom. She closed the door and leaned against it.

So that was that. Nick had acknowledged that he considered last night a mistake and now they were to go on from there. She was to forget about what had happened as though she had dreamed the whole sequence. They would wait for the situation at the office to come to fruition and then end the marriage.

She leaned against the door, tears sliding unnoticed down her face. Boy, had they ever managed to destroy a friendship. Maybe she could write a book about it someday. "Don't ever marry a friend. It will destroy the relationship."

Dani turned on the shower. She needed to get a grip on herself and her emotions. She had planned to work this afternoon. Thank God. Her work had always been her salvation. Today was no exception.

Nick stared at the closed door, wondering what he could have said differently. He'd made a mess of everything. He had decided not to put any pressure on her until the situation at her work was resolved. Then he had intended to court her, to convince her that what they shared was enough to make a long-lasting happy relationship.

And he'd blown it.

He found his socks and shoes and sat down in one of the chairs to put them on. When he was dressed Nick continued to stare out the window, seeing nothing but his lost dreams.

The next few weeks went by with their established routine at home. Dani continued to put in long hours at the office and Nick worked on the idea he had for a novel. Outwardly nothing had changed. They were both polite, even cordial, with each other.

But Nick no longer teased Dani and Dani seemed to have withdrawn into some place inside herself where the impulsive woman Nick knew was hidden away.

Nick and Dani had been married for two months when a breakthrough happened in the formula Frank and Dani had been working on for so long. They were ecstatic. The ensuing celebration in the lab with all the assistants was one of hilarity.

Dani was very late coming home that night.

She tiptoed into the bedroom. Nick was sound asleep but the covers looked as though he'd been in a wrestling match. She wasn't sure who'd won. She had intended to tell him that the case was nearing completion. As soon as she had reached home, she called the special number that she had memorized long ago and reported what had happened.

She had hoped the authorities would confront Frank before this point in their experiments, but in a way she was glad he had been a part of this success. He was an excellent lab partner. Regardless of what he had done in the past, what he was still doing, she knew she was going to miss working with him.

How many times had she wanted to ask him why he was doing this to himself, to his career, to the company? But of course she hadn't.

Surely the authorities had enough information on him by now to arrest him.

After changing in the bathroom, Dani tiptoed into the bedroom and carefully got into bed. Nick hadn't moved.

She hadn't realized how tired she was until she was lying down. She closed her eyes and sighed. She would tell Nick in the morning.

But by the time she awakened in the morning he was already locked away in his office. Dani always respected that closed door. Today would be no exception. She would have to wait.

Dani drove to work, her heart heavy. How could so much have gone wrong in such a short time? She and Nick were like strangers living together, and yet it was much worse because now she had the memory of their night at the Plaza to haunt her.

She still ached with the thought that he was sorry for what had happened. Dani couldn't be sorry because it was one of the most moving experiences she'd ever had.

When she got to work she greeted Frank with a brief smile.

"Too much celebrating last night, I take it?" he asked, looking a little heavy-eyed himself.

"Not really. I just had some trouble sleeping."

He sighed, removed his glasses and polished them absently. "If you're like me, it's a letdown even though we've been successful. We know there's going to be months of testing, but that's not the same as the excitement of the search."

Dani sat down at her computer and turned it on. Frank followed her. "Dani, there's something I need to tell you. I couldn't before, but now that—"

The door to the lab opened and Mr. Worthington walked in with two men. Dani recognized them but she hadn't seen them since that

Saturday so many weeks ago when she'd first gone to Nick's home.

So much had happened to her since then that she felt like another person.

Frank turned to Mr. Worthington and smiled. "Good morning. I see you received my memo about our newest findings."

Mr. Worthington nodded. "Frank, these gentlemen are here to speak with you and Dani. I have assured them both of you will cooperate." He looked at the other men. "Adams, I'll turn this over to you."

The older of the two agents nodded and stepped forward. His eyes on Frank, he said, "I understand you're having some family problems, Mr. Dekin."

Dani watched Frank stiffen, his color fading. He looked at the three men. "I don't know what you're talking about. Who are you?"

"My name is Sam Adams," he replied, pulling out his identification. "My partner and I are with the F.B.I. We've had you under surveillance for the past few months."

Frank fumbled for a chair and sank into it. "Then you already know," he murmured, as though talking to himself.

"Why don't you start from the beginning, Frank?"

"I received a phone call—" he lifted his hand, then dropped it "—I don't know when. I was told that my parents had been removed from their home, along with my sister who only recently graduated from high school."

He looked up at the men watching him, then glanced at Dani. "I was promised that if I cooperated they would not be harmed and that I would be able to talk with them once a week. But I wouldn't be able to see them."

"They were being held as hostages?"

"Yes."

"For what?"

"They knew that I worked in a high-security job. Whoever these men are, they understand enough about the semiconductor industry to know that a process such as the one we've been researching would prove to be invaluable." He shrugged. "In exchange for my family, they wanted the formula."

"Why didn't you go to the police?"

"Because I had nothing concrete to tell them. According to my parents' neighbors and my sister's friends, they had decided to take a long trip. No one was certain how long they would be gone or seemed to be concerned about their absence." He looked down at his hands. "All I had to verify what they told me were the weekly phone calls."

"Were they long-distance?"

"I couldn't tell. Sometimes the line was very clear. Other times there was static."

"Did your family pass on any clue?"

"If they did I couldn't tell what it was." Dani could hear the frustration in his voice. "They insisted they were not being mistreated. We were never allowed to talk more than a few moments."

"Were you asked to report your progress?"

He nodded. "Periodically I would send a printout of what we were working on to a post-office box in New York City."

Dani glanced up and saw the two agents exchange glances. Adams raised his brows slightly and his partner gave a brief nod.

"You knew at that time that you were selling company secrets, did you not?" Adams asked.

"I didn't feel as though I was selling anything. I never received any money. Only the assurance that my family would pay the consequences if I didn't give every appearance of cooperating. But I never gave them anything of value."

"Would you care to explain?"

"I made up a dummy set of formulas, close enough to the real one that even an expert in the field would believe it, unless he or she tried to duplicate our findings. In order to do that, they would need a laboratory as sophisticated as this one. There aren't that many in the world."

"What did you intend to do once you completed your research?"

"Send them the final data, carefully inaccurate, and get my family back. Then I was going to the authorities."

"Either that, or you intended to sell what you have and retire down south. I understand Brazil is quite nice at this time of year."

Frank shrugged. "You can believe what you like."

"Yes, we can," Adams agreed. "We're placing you under arrest." He began reading Frank his rights while Dani, Mr. Worthington and the other agent stood by. Dani felt disoriented. How could all this be happening so quickly after having taken so long to get to this point?

Even after Frank left with the two agents, she continued to sit there, staring blankly at the door.

"You did the right thing, Dani," Mr. Worthington said quietly.

"How did you know that was what I was thinking?"

"Because I understand. You and Frank have worked well together for some time. You enjoyed each other's company enough to spend your social time with him. I know how difficult all of this must have been for you."

"If he'd only told me."

"If he had, you would have been implicated, as well." He sat down in the chair next to hers. "You see, Dani, he had the same choice you did. He could have come to me immediately, explained what had happened and allowed me to decide how to handle it."

She nodded. "I'm sure you're right. I wonder why he didn't?"

"He wasn't thinking. He was just reacting."

Dani recalled her panic the night she had run to Nick. It hadn't occurred to her to call Mr. Worthington that night. It had taken Nick's prompting. How would she have behaved if the call had been about *her* parents? She would like to think that she would have done the right thing, but she honestly didn't know how she would have responded to such a threat. Thank God she had been able to turn to Nick.

Frank didn't have someone like Nick in his life, someone to turn to in times of stress and trouble. Although they were friends, Frank hadn't trusted her with what had happened. Why should he? He may have actually considered it and decided not to involve her.

Or was his story a total fabrication? She wondered if she would ever hear what happened.

Surely sooner or later she would be asked to make a statement in the case.

She dropped her head into her hands. Would Frank find out that she had reported him? She wasn't sure she could face him, even though she had never really had a choice in the matter, and be able to live with herself.

"Why don't you go home, take a few days off, and try to recuperate from the strain I know you've been under?"

She nodded. "Thanks. I haven't been sleeping well lately."

Mr. Worthington patted her hand. "That's understandable. I want you to know how much I appreciate what you've done, Dani. I know how difficult all of this must have been for you."

"Yes. Yes, it was."

She gathered up her purse and jacket, and started toward the door. It was over. All of it. She could go home and tell Nick. Dani felt numb, but she knew that eventually she would experience the relief of having all of this behind her.

She would pick up the pieces of her life, the way they were before the investigation had begun. No doubt Nick would be pleased to get his life back in order, without her always underfoot.

Dani drove home slowly, recognizing to her dismay that telling Nick that the reason for their marriage no longer existed would be one of the most difficult things she'd ever had to do.

Chapter Eleven

When Dani reached Nick's home she pulled into the driveway and sat there, looking at the house. It was surrounded by trees and couldn't be seen from the road. Like Nick, the house was private, willing to share its secrets with only a select and chosen group.

Dani had always felt as though she were a part of that special circle, but lately she had discovered how difficult it was to feel close to Nick when he obviously didn't want her to draw any nearer than she already had.

She let herself into the kitchen and smiled at the housekeeper.

"Why, Mrs. Montgomery, what are you doing here at this time of day?"

Dani hadn't realized how tired she was until she'd reached home. "I've decided to take some time off." She glanced at her watch. "Somehow I managed to forget to eat. Is there anything left over from Nick's lunch?"

"Oh, he wasn't hungry. I have some soup I could heat up for you and some freshly baked bread."

"Is Nick writing?"

"I don't think so. The last time I saw him he was in the den."

"I'll go find him. Maybe he's ready to eat now."

Dani paused in the doorway of the den, surprised to see the draperies closed. The room was in deep shadow and she discovered Nick sitting in one of the overstuffed lounging chairs, facing the empty fireplace.

Quietly she walked over to him. If he was asleep she didn't want to disturb him. When she drew near he turned his head and looked at her.

"It's over, isn't it?" he asked in a low voice.

She nodded. "They arrested Frank this morning." She described the events of the past few hours to him. "It was even more difficult than I could have imagined," she said when she had finished relating what had happened. "You see,

I believe him. That's why I was so upset. I just could not understand why Frank would willingly betray our work. He's not that type of person."

Nick heard the conviction in her voice and fought to hold his composure. Perhaps Dani didn't realize what she was revealing about her feelings toward Frank. She was in love with the man. It couldn't be any plainer to him than if she had come in shouting the news.

Why shouldn't she be? She and Frank had so much in common. Their shared interests far outweighed anything Nick could offer her.

He leaned his head back and closed his eyes.

"Nick, aren't you feeling well?"

That's one way of putting it, he thought. "I have a headache."

"That's probably because you've been working too hard and not eating. Dorothy tells me you didn't eat anything for lunch. What don't you join me now? I'm having some soup."

He didn't answer right away. He kept his eyes closed and Dani took advantage of the opportunity to just sit there and look at him. She hadn't realized until she'd been driving home how often he managed lately to avoid being around her. Looking at him now, she discovered that he seemed tired, his face drawn, with shadows beneath his eyes.

Obviously their present situation had been as difficult for him as it was for her. He'd probably be relieved to have her out of his life.

She was determined not to allow her personal feelings for him to sway what she knew she must do—and that was to allow him the space to get on with his life. He'd done enough for her. He'd sacrificed the past few months of his life. That was enough.

After several minutes of silence Nick opened his eyes and looked at her. She held out her hand. "Let's get something to eat," she said softly. "Afterwards I propose we both take a nap. I don't know about you, but I haven't been sleeping well lately." She hoped her tone was light enough.

"I know," he responded, reluctantly taking her hand and coming to his feet. They walked toward the kitchen, hand in hand.

"Oh, I'm sorry if I've kept you awake."

"You've had a lot on your mind. We both have."

She nodded. "Thank God it's finally over."

He didn't respond. Dorothy smiled at them both when they walked into the kitchen. "Good. You managed to convince him, did you?" She motioned to the table. "Sit down and eat."

Dani realized after several more minutes of silence that unless she initiated conversation, they were going to sit across from each other during their meal without saying a word.

"How's your writing coming?"

He glanced up, then gave a slight shrug. "Sometimes the words flow, but I'm not at all sure I'm saying much. Other times I have to fight for every word and I still can't tell if it's worth saving."

She took a bite of food before she responded. "That's the way my work has been going lately. Mr. Worthington said I probably needed some time off. I decided to take him up on his offer."

"What are your plans now?"

She smiled. "I haven't made any past taking a long leisurely nap." She smiled. "I hope you intend to join me. Rest would probably be the best thing you can do for your headache."

He glanced away. Then he looked back at her. As though coming to some decision, he replied, "Why not?"

They finished their meal and went to the bedroom. Dani went into the bathroom, shed her clothes and stepped under the steaming shower.

After she'd dried herself she slipped into the robe she kept hanging behind the door and returned to the bedroom. Nick had turned the covers back, taken off his clothes and was already in bed, his back turned away from her.

Quietly she crawled into the other side. The food and the shower had helped to relax her and within minutes she was asleep.

When she finally surfaced, she was in Nick's arms. He held her firmly against him, his face buried in her tousled curls.

This must be what heaven is like, Dani decided dreamily. She placed a kiss just beneath Nick's ear. She could still smell the slight scent of his after-shave. She placed another kiss, light and very soft, against his ear, then another along his jaw line, another...

He groaned, as though in pain.

"Nick?" she whispered. "Are you all right?" She placed her hand on his chest. He was definitely warm. "Does your head hurt?"

He took her hand and guided it down his body. "Not my head, Dani," was his rueful response.

Touching him gave her so much pleasure that she smiled—and ran her other hand down his spine. He turned his head slightly and she found his mouth.

Nick wanted her, that was plain enough for even Dani, with her lack of experience, to determine. She no longer cared that the events of the day had changed their situation. All she knew was that she was with Nick, that she loved him more than she had ever thought it possible to love anyone, and that he wanted her.

For the moment that was enough.

She felt as though she was still asleep, still dreaming about Nick, free to indulge all of her fantasies, because none of this was really happening. She knew she would wake up and discover that once again her dreams had fooled her.

Since what was happening wasn't real, Dani allowed her aggressive nature to take over. She nudged Nick over until he lay on his back, then began to kiss him, to touch him, to explore the muscles and planes of his body.

She loved to touch his chest, to feel the soft curls that covered the wide expanse. She ran her tongue across his flat nipple and felt his body jerk in reaction. Dani lost track of everything but her own enjoyment as she kissed and caressed every inch of his body.

At one point he reached for her curls, running his fingers through them, kneading her scalp as she delicately touched him. She smiled to herself at the almost inaudible sounds he made from time to time in response to what she was doing.

Then he could take no more. He rolled, pinning her beneath him. Blindly he sought her mouth with his. She opened to him, accepting and encouraging him to possess her. When he did, she sighed with relief and pleasure.

Nick held her tightly, almost desperately, as though he never intended to let her go. He teased and tantalized her until she could stand no more, her body suddenly convulsing around him, drawing him even closer to her. Nick gave a final lunge, gasping, then lay still, still clutching her to him.

Dani smiled to herself, enjoying her dream, and drifted off to sleep once more.

When she awoke, the room was in deep shadow, and she realized she had slept through the entire afternoon. She looked over to Nick's side of the bed, but he wasn't there. She stretched and smiled. What a wonderful sleep she'd had. And her dreams! They almost made her blush.

She sat up and discovered that her robe had come undone. She pulled it around her and slipped out of bed, wondering how Nick's headache was. She hoped his nap had helped him as much as hers had rejuvenated her.

Dani slipped into some casual clothes and went in search of Nick. He wasn't hard to find. He stood looking out the window of the den, his hands in his pockets.

"You should have awakened me. I didn't mean to sleep all afternoon."

Slowly he turned and looked at her. "You needed your rest."

She laughed. "I must admit that I feel better than I have for some time."

Nick would have to say that she looked more alive, more glowing than he had seen her look for several weeks. It was obvious that the strain of the situation at work had taken its toll.

He leaned against the wall by the window. "What are your plans now?"

She walked over to him and hugged him. He stiffened and Dani reluctantly stepped back. Was he afraid she was going to cling to him now that there was no need to continue the marriage? Well, he was wrong. She'd depended on him long enough. It was time for her to show him that she had finally grown up, emotionally as well as physically.

She seated herself on the sofa and smiled at him. "I think I'm going to just be lazy for a few days, take it easy." She wished she could read the expression on his face but it was no use. He was keeping it purposely blank. "I need to look for another apartment of course. But that shouldn't take long. I might check the complex where I used to live and see if any vacancies have occurred since I left."

Nick walked over and sat down across from her. "That really isn't necessary, you know," he said in a careful voice.

"I think it is, Nick. You've lived up to your part of the agreement. Now it's my turn to live up to mine. You've been very patient with me.

You have no idea how much your friendship means to me." For a moment it looked to Dani as though he had flinched at the word *friendship*, but the movement was so slight she could have been mistaken.

She smiled at him, knowing that she had to be strong to get through this. "I've loved being here with you. You've been wonderful to me and I appreciate it very much." She paused because her throat seemed to be clogging up with the words she didn't want to have to say. She took a deep breath and forced herself to continue. "I need to get on with my life and learn to look to myself for answers instead of always running to you whenever I get myself in trouble."

"I'll always be here for you, Dani. You know that." His voice was so low she barely heard him.

She nodded. "I know," she whispered hoarsely.

"What are we going to tell our families?"

"I haven't gotten that far in my plans. Do we have to tell them anything at the moment?"

"They're going to have to know sometime, Dani," he pointed out in a gentle voice.

She bit her bottom lip. "Let's wait a few weeks, though." She was quiet for a few moments, then said, "I don't suppose there's any reason not to tell them the truth, now. What do you think?"

"You'd better clear that with the authorities first."

She nodded. "That's true." She sighed. "It's still so complicated, isn't it?"

For a brief moment she wanted to throw herself at him and beg him to allow her to stay. But she recognized that the child within her was still battling to have her own way. That was the problem with children. They were so self-centered, never looking at anyone's needs or desires but their own.

She came to her feet and held out her hands to Nick. "Thank you for being a part of my life, Nick. It wouldn't have been the same without you."

He took her hands and squeezed them. "I'm glad I could help."

She nodded. "Well." She looked around the room as though searching for something. "What do we do now?"

Nick stood. "As a matter of fact I need to pack."

"Pack? What do you mean?"

"I guess I forgot to mention a call I received from my agent this morning. I need to fly out to L.A. for another story conference. I booked a flight leaving late tonight, so that I'll be there first thing in the morning."

"Oh. How long will you be gone?"

He shrugged. "Who knows? I may be back in a couple of days. Or it may be a couple of weeks, depending on how the meetings go."

She turned away. "I'll probably be gone by then."

"There's no rush in your moving out, is there?"

"There's no reason to prolong my stay, either."

They both waited for the other to say something more, something to stop this calamity from happening, but neither one could think of anything else to say. They had made an agreement. They would abide by that agreement, despite any personal feelings to the contrary. Dani knew she could not in good conscience expect more of Nick than what he'd already given her.

Dani offered to drive Nick to the airport. He thought about the inconvenience of having to find a ride back home when he returned, but weighed against the fact that he would be able to spend a little more time with Dani, he agreed.

She went inside the airport terminal and waited with him until his flight was announced. When the line started forming to board Nick turned to her. "Take care of yourself, okay?"

She nodded.

He pulled her into his arms and kissed her. She clung to him, knowing that the next time she saw him things would be so different, knowing that this man had taught her so much about herself and about love. He had accepted her and loved her just the way she was.

When he finally released her, tears smudged her cheeks. "Hey, what's this?" His finger touched her cheek.

Her smile was more than a little wobbly. "I always cry at airports. It's traditional."

"Dani," he replied with wry humor, "you've never done anything traditional in your life."

"Sure I have. I married the boy next door, didn't I? I got married in my mother's wedding gown. What's more traditional than that?"

"Somehow the way you go about doing traditional things is very untraditional."

"And you're going to miss your plane if you don't board now."

"Thank you for bringing me to the airport."

All Dani wanted to do was get away from him now before she broke down. Was he going to let her go before she made a complete fool of herself? She'd never been good at saying goodbye, particularly when it was said to Nick.

This time she was also saying goodbye to the man she now knew she would love for the rest of her life, the man no other man could possibly replace.

"It was the least I could do for you, Nick. The very least." But to herself, she added, *The hardest thing I've ever had to do for you is to give you your freedom. I hope I can survive the experience.*

She watched him stride to the opening of the ramp into the jet and hand the waiting attendant his ticket. He glanced back and waved. Dani forced herself to smile, as though she didn't feel her heart splintering into a thousand pieces in her chest, and wave back.

And then he was gone.

She tried to keep her mind blank as she went back to the car. She forced herself to think about anything but Nick on the drive home. When she opened the front door Muffin sat on the bottom step of the stairway waiting for her.

Dani burst into tears.

Muffin had accepted their move the way he accepted everything in life—with feline indifference. His routine was set. He spent his evenings in search of female companionship, coming in mornings to eat and sleep, no doubt savoring the dreams of his past exploits and future hopes. But somehow he must have known that she would need him tonight.

She walked over and sat down on the step beside him. He immediately jumped into her lap and nudged her hand with his head. Absently she stroked behind each ear while the tears continued to roll down her cheeks.

"Isn't this the silliest thing you've ever seen me do, Muff? Why am I crying over Nick? Nothing has really changed, has it? We haven't fought. It isn't as though we're never going to see each other again.

"But how can I go back to the way things were before? How can I forget about his lovemaking? I—"

She paused, startled at the memory of something. She had awakened some time during her afternoon to find Nick holding her. That had been no dream. On some level she had known that, but it had been easier to face him later if she pretended that what they had shared earlier had not happened.

He had already made his feelings clear on the subject, so she had blocked what had happened out of her conscious mind. She hugged Muffin to her, only to release him when he complained. Muffin licked her hand to show he had no hard feelings.

Nick had wanted her and, on some level, had needed her. She couldn't remember Nick ever needing anyone. She sighed, stroking Muffin. But his need had only been temporary, a physical desire easily assuaged.

Wearily she stood, Muffin still in her arms, and walked into the bedroom. Tomorrow would be soon enough to look for a place to live. Tonight she was too exhausted to think about what she needed to do. The thought of packing did not trigger any anticipation within her.

It would be easier to do what had to be done without Nick here. Already she missed him, and she realized that this was the first time since their wedding that they'd been separated overnight. For the past three months they had slept together, shared the same room and bath, set up a routine that worked for them. They'd become a couple without consciously planning to do so.

If she'd known how painful it would be to get on with her life Dani would never have allowed Nick to convince her that marriage was a necessary part of their plans.

She placed Muffin on the bed, found her nightgown and undressed. When she came out of the bathroom after brushing her teeth she discovered Muffin still sitting where she'd left him.

"Do you want outside?"

He stared at her for a long moment before finally blinking. Then he lifted a paw, examined it, and daintily touched it with his tongue.

"I take it that's a no," she muttered. She crawled into bed and turned out the light. Never had she been so aware of the gigantic size of that bed. She felt a movement by her hip, a soft purr, and Muffin sprawled out alongside her.

She began to cry—deep painful sobs that forced their way to the surface from some well of pain inside of her. Instinctively Muffin had known that she needed him tonight, the comfort of knowing that she wasn't alone.

Dani knew that she would get through this. It was just that, at the moment, she didn't know how.

Chapter Twelve

First days later, Dani had found another apartment, paid her deposit and first month's rent and had no more reason to stay at Nick's house.

She knew that she had hoped he would be home before now or at the very least he might call.

He hadn't.

So today she would pack her things and move them to her new place.

She had been in touch with Mr. Worthington, who told her that much of what Frank had told them had already been known to the authorities and that the place where his family was being held had been under surveillance. They hadn't been sure that the family members were being held against their will, and they'd been waiting to see if Frank had hidden his family away himself.

But when the arrests were made, two of the men involved explained that they had been hired to watch the family. They weren't told why.

The mysterious line of communication was traced to a man on the West Coast who was currently working on a similar project to the one Frank and Dani had been on. Frank's changes in the formula had bought time for the authorities to trace the plan back to its originator, but without Dani's intervention, they would not have had a chance to set up their surveillance network.

Frank had gambled on the thieves not being able to figure out what was wrong, but with the information he was giving them, the man on the West Coast had been adjusting the formula, looking for the correct one. It had only been a matter of time before he would have found it.

Mr. Worthington didn't know what would become of Frank's case. He would be tried and, because of the evidence, no doubt convicted. It was up to the court to decide what would happen to him after that.

Dani had given a great deal of thought to whether or not to attempt to see Frank, and she'd finally decided not to do so. Instead she sent him a short letter, wishing him well under the circumstances.

Frank would never know how the decisions he'd made had triggered a whole series of events unrelated to him.

All the while she packed, she thought of how each person's life affects another's. She liked Frank and she accepted the fact that he had done what he thought he had to do. So had she. Now she had to live with the consequences of her decisions, just as Frank was living with the consequences of his.

At last her car was loaded and Dani went back into the house, making one last check before leaving. Thank God Dorothy had the day off. Dani hadn't been in the mood for explanations.

Dani found herself standing in the doorway of Nick's office. She had never gone in there before. Not because he'd told her to stay away, but because she had always respected his privacy. But on this particular occasion Dani wanted to feel Nick's presence. It was never so much in evidence as it was in this room.

She walked in and looked around. The room was small, rather cozy and filled with book shelves. She wandered over to the shelves. So much of Nick was on display. There were pictures of him growing up. Pictures of him at college and later when his first play was produced.

She picked up a ceramic sculpture that she hadn't thought about in years. She'd made it in an art class in the seventh grade, and had given it to Nick for Christmas that year. As she recalled, it was supposed to be a dog, like the one he'd had when he was a boy, but there was little resemblance between the two. She hadn't realized how truly awful it was, but she clearly recalled how Nick had thanked her for it. The face was lopsided and one ear was misshapen and the silly thing had the most undoglike expression anyone could imagine.

But he had kept it all these years.

She found her senior picture from high school next to one of the two of them taken at the beach when she was fifteen. Group pictures generally included her, which wasn't surprising. She had tagged along behind him for years.

But no more. He had his own life to lead. It was time for her to let go.

Dani turned away and started out of the room, but paused. There were some papers scattered on his desk and she wondered if this was part of what he was working on at the moment. Curiosity won out and she walked over to the desk and picked up the first sheet.

As she read she began to tremble, her legs shaking so much that she sank into the chair. Nick had written this, that was obvious. But when? And why hadn't he told her?

She was five years old the first time I saw her, but she looked even younger. She was crying and seemed so forlorn that I found myself going up to her to see what I could do to help. I will never forget the shock of looking into those big black oh-so-sad eyes and knowing that I never wanted to see that expression on her face again. I knew at that moment that I would always do whatever I had to do to keep the sadness at bay.

At ten, my vow was unconscious. Twenty years later I realize that my vow is the same, and very conscious this time. I cannot stand to see Dani in pain and I will always do whatever necessary to chase the sadness from her eyes.

We lived next door to each other, Dani and me, from the time she was five and I was ten. I don't remember much about the first ten years of my life. I'm sure I did all the usual things a boy does growing up. I don't remember anything traumatic happening during that time. I just lived day to day, I'm sure. But whenever I think of my childhood, Dani always pops into my memory, as though I truly began to live the day I found her sitting on her front steps, crying. I'll never forget those big black eyes staring at me, or the way her baby-fine black hair looked in tousled curls around her face and ears.

I lost my boyish heart at that moment and never missed it. I didn't understand what had happened to me at the time. It took many years and I suppose some growing up on my part to truly understand what Dani means to me.

She was the catalyst that kept me moving, growing, exploring, learning and fighting. Yes, Dani was the cause of a great many fights in my young life, both with her and with other people. Boy, could she set off my temper. I got teased about her during those years. I got teased a lot. And I hated it. Or at least I thought I did.

The thing was, Dani was as much a part of my life as eating, sleeping or going to school. She was part of the air I breathed. I just didn't know it.

Until now. I see the pain in her eyes and know that this time, I'm the one who put it there. I'm the one who, in my arrogance, believed I knew what was best for her.

It took me twenty years to recognize that I love Dani in every way a man can love a woman. Why did I think I could convince her that she loved me in the same way?

Oh, I know. If anyone had asked me six months ago, I would have explained that Dani was like a little sister to me—a pest, at times, but lovable. Who would have guessed that my feelings had continued to grow until they exploded into a confusion of emotion? I wanted to protect her, all right. But I wanted so much more. I wanted to live with her, make love to her, give her children, claim her in every way a man can claim a woman. She was mine. She always had been. Didn't she understand that?

Of course not. And why should she? Just because I'd been so slow in understanding my feelings didn't mean that she shared those feelings.

The night at the Plaza was the biggest mistake I could have ever made. I know that now. Before I could only fantasize about what it would be like to make love to Dani. After that night I knew too well the power-

ful and profound feelings I'd unleashed in my arrogant ignorance.

I have paid for my actions every day since then, lying awake beside her night after night, wanting to touch her and knowing that if I did I would lose what little control I've managed to hang on to.

I've watched her become more and more quiet around me, watched her restless sleep at night, knowing full well that I'm the one who trapped her into this situation.

I thought I could teach her to love me in the way I wanted. What a laugh! It's just that, at the moment, I'm having a little trouble finding the humor in the situation. I deserve what I'm feeling for ever thinking I could force her into a situation that I knew I wanted to make permanent, all the while convincing her the marriage would only be temporary.

Why couldn't I have been more honest with her? Even now I find myself rehearsing ways to tell her about the way I feel. But for what reason? So she will take pity on me?

I don't want her pity. I would rather hang on to what we have, at least keep the friendship, than to cause her additional pain when she is unable to give me anything more.

Dani sat staring at the papers in her hands in shock. Why hadn't Nick told her?

But he had, a little voice reminded her. How many times had he told her that he loved her? How many ways had he shown her how much?

How could she have been so incredibly obtuse?

So many of his moods in recent weeks were explained. She had attributed his behavior to his impatience with the current situation. Impatience had been only one of the emotions he'd been battling.

The question now was what did she intend to do about it? She stared at the pages in front of her. How many wives of three months suddenly discover that the man they married loves them and wants to have a permanent relationship? These things were generally worked out at an earlier stage.

But as Nick had pointed out, nothing she did was ever traditional. And yet he loved her anyway.

All right. She would treat this like a problem in the lab. She knew the results she was looking for. The question was how to find them?

Somehow she intended to prove to Nick that her love for him was as strong as his was for her. Starting now.

It was almost two in the morning when the cab let Nick out in his driveway. Nick felt as though he hadn't slept during the week he'd been gone. He hated cross-country traveling. Not only was it tiring at the time, it also took his body a few days to adjust to the time change.

The driveway was empty and he realized that unconsciously he had hoped Dani would still be there. Once again he reminded himself that she had to get on with her life. There was no reason for her to hang around now. No doubt it had been easier for both of them for her to leave while he was gone. He didn't think he could have calmly watched as she packed her belongings without giving way to the desire to hold her and explain how much he needed her in his life.

A scene like that would have ended up embarrassing both of them. No. Everything had happened the way it should.

For now.

Nick had done quite a lot of thinking while he was gone. He'd turned down several invitations to spend the evenings with business associates. On one occasion he'd seen Letitia. She'd been friendly, glad to see him, and had even invited him over for dinner one night, but he had used a rushed schedule as an excuse to decline.

He knew now what he intended to do about Dani. The first step had been to let her go, to give her a sense of freedom and space. They had concluded their agreement as planned.

Now he intended to pursue her with no hindrance from any agreement he might have made.

He loved Dani and he knew she loved him. All he had to do was to convince her that she loved him enough to stay married to him.

The way she had responded to him the times they had made love gave him hope. Each night he had been gone he'd relived their final afternoon together, allowing himself to find encouragement in the fact that she had responded so aggressively toward him. He'd been afraid to mention their lovemaking that night at the airport for fear she would think he was trying to trap her into staying.

No, they had needed the time apart with no pressure.

He'd told her to leave her new address and phone number for him if she moved out before he returned. He would call her when he woke up tomorrow, as he had promised. He'd offer to take her to dinner, whatever she wanted to do.

He'd start dropping by to see her evenings, keep her company.

Maybe he'd discuss the possibility of her postponing seeing a lawyer for a while. They didn't have to live together anymore, not if she didn't want to live with him, but there was no reason to make any rash decisions about finalizing the separation.

Nick let himself into the dark house and set his suitcase just inside the door. He'd worry about it tomorrow. As he started down the hallway he began to peel off his clothes, leaving them wherever they happened to fall.

He walked into the bedroom and headed straight for the bed. Dear God, but he was tired! He was asleep by the time his head hit the pillow.

The dream came to him again, the same one that had haunted him every night he'd been in L.A. He and Dani had flown to some south-sea island, a place where no one else had ever been— a tropical paradise just made for two.

He watched Dani, night after night, as she cavorted in the waves of the turquoise blue water, her black hair and eyes a stark contrast to her fair skin.

During one dream a shark suddenly swam past her. She had screamed and Nick had run toward her, splashing through the shallow water and whisking her off her feet. He'd taken her to the edge of the white glistening sand, beneath the gently swaying palm trees, and placed her on a woven mat.

Another night a giant octopus had waved menacing tentacles toward her, but Nick had managed to rescue her.

Tonight there was no threat that he could sense. He was free to watch Dani enjoy the sand, the sun and the surf. Eventually he decided to join her.

He splashed toward her. When she saw him coming she laughed and turned away. She began to swim out into the lagoon and he followed her until he finally caught up with her.

She still laughed at him as he caught her to him, and hugged her.

"I love you, Dani."

"I know you do, Nick. You're my best friend in all the world."

"I don't want to be your best friend anymore. Don't you understand? I want to be your husband. Your lover."

Dani laughed gaily. "But of course. You're all those things, Nick. Friend, husband, lover."

"Don't leave me, Dani."

"How could I possibly do that? And why would I want to? Don't you understand? I love you. I love you. I..."

Nick woke up, muttering the same phrase, over and over. Then he turned over and drifted off to sleep once again.

The jangling of the phone roused him hours later. He fought his way out of a sleep-caused fog and grabbed the receiver.

"Hello?"

"Oh, Nick, thank God you're there! I didn't know if you'd be back from L.A. or not, but I just took a chance that—"

Nick sat up, clutching the phone with both hands. "Dani? Dani, are you okay? What's wrong? Where are you?"

"I'm in Florida and I—"

"Florida! What in the hell are you doing down there?"

"Please don't get upset, Nick. I know I told you I'd never bother you again. It's just—"

"No, no. That's all right. I'm glad you called. Really. I had planned to call you first thing this morning, but I guess I overslept." He glanced at his watch. It was almost eleven. "What's wrong, Dani?"

"I decided to use some of my vacation time to get away. There's so many decisions that need to be made that I thought getting away for a while might help.''

''Makes sense.''

''Well, when I flew down here I noticed this man seated a couple of rows ahead of me.''

''Who is he? Do you know him?''

''I don't think so. I guess I'm just so jumpy these days. It's probably nothing. I wouldn't have thought much about it, but this morning I discovered that he's staying in the same hotel. I—''

''Now, Dani, listen to me. I want you to stay right there, do you hear me? Don't leave your room for any reason. I'll catch the first plane out of here and get there as soon as I can.''

''I don't think there's any real danger or anything,'' she said in a hesitant voice.

''I agree. But you never know. When you get hungry, call room service, but make damn sure it's room service before you open the door.'' He grabbed a pen and the small spiral notebook that lay by the phone. ''Now tell me where you are. I'll get there as soon as I can.''

Hours later Nick was airborne. He settled back into his seat with a sigh. Once again he was rushing off to take care of Dani.

He grinned. So she still needed him. She'd been frightened and he was the one she had called. That suited him just fine.

As soon as he arrived at the resort hotel Nick crossed the immense lobby and approached the front desk.

"May I help you, sir?"

"Yes. My name is Nick Montgomery and I—"

"Ah, yes, Mr. Montgomery. Your wife said that you were expected this evening." The clerk handed him a security card enclosed in an envelope. "Your room number is written on the envelope. Just place the card in the slot of the door and watch for the red light. As soon as it blinks, you have a few seconds to open the door before it relocks."

"Thanks."

He glanced at the number. 1501. Her room must be near the top of the hotel. When he stepped into the elevator he noted that the fifteenth floor was in fact the top floor.

There were only two doors with numbers on them when he stepped off the elevator. He walked over to the one marked 1501, stuck the card in, then turned the handle.

The room he walked into caused him to pause in disbelief. It looked like it belonged on a Hollywood set. Wide areas of glass overlooked the beach on one side, while the second glass wall revealed a terrace. The furniture was the latest in style, comfort and luxury. Double doors at one end of the room beckoned to him. When he opened them he found an opulent bedroom. The terrace extended along one side of the room. What in the world was Dani doing in a place like this? For that matter, where was she? Hadn't he told her not to leave? Hadn't he warned her that... He heard a sound coming from yet another door. The sound of water trickling. Perhaps she was in the bathroom.

Nick found Dani in a tub large enough to seat four to six people. The water gently bubbled and churned around her, causing the foam to conceal most of her from view.

She lay stretched out, her head resting on a pillow at the edge of the tub. Several lit candles provided the only illumination, but because of the mirrored walls, the light was reflected over and over, making the room look surrealistic.

"Dani?"

She opened her eyes and saw him standing there. Her lips curved into a warm smile. "Hello, Nick."

He was having trouble adjusting his imagined picture of her cowering in the corner of some tiny hotel room, frantically waiting for his arrival, to the reality before him. All the questions that had been running through his mind sounded ridiculous at this particular moment. *Are you all right?* had been one of the first ones. She certainly looked to be in sublime condition. *Are you frightened?* sounded even more asinine.

"Why don't you join me?" she asked.

"What's going on?"

Her eyes widened innocently. "I thought I'd enjoy the hot tub while I was waiting for you to get here."

This was not the voice of the woman who'd awakened him earlier in the day. When he continued to stand there staring at her she slowly came to her feet. The bubbles fell away from her body as the water receded from her shoulders, her breasts, her waist, her—

"Dani!"

She paused. "I thought I'd help you undress."

"I, uh, think that I can manage on my own," he responded, absently reaching for the buttons of his shirt.

She sank back into the water. "Whatever you say."

What was the matter with her? He'd never seen her in this sort of mood before. Her idea of getting away for a vacation must have been a good one to have created such a change in her.

The water *did* look enticing, he had to admit. He removed his shirt, pants, socks and briefs and stepped in beside her. For the first time since he had left her over a week ago Nick could feel himself relaxing.

"Why did you call me, Dani?"

"Because I needed you."

"Have you seen the man on the plane again?"

"Of course not. I stayed in my room all day, just as you recommended."

"But he was watching you, right?"

She thought about that for a few moments. "I don't think so."

"Then what frightened you about him?"

She met his gaze. "I never said that he frightened me. All I managed to tell you was that I saw a man on the plane and later discovered he was staying at this hotel. Before I could say anything else you were insisting I stay locked in my room until you got here. Of course I obeyed." She smiled. "Don't I always do what you tell me to do?"

While she was talking Dani had slid her foot from his ankle to his knee. He grabbed her foot before she moved it any higher.

"Maybe you'd better tell me what it was about the man you saw that made you call me this morning."

Her smile widened. "I think he was on his honeymoon and I got to thinking about the fact that you and I never had a honeymoon. But it's very difficult going on a honeymoon by yourself. You told me to call you if I ever needed you." Her fingers trailed along his thigh. "So I did."

"You needed me for a honeymoon?" he managed to say in a strangled voice.

"I know it's traditional for the groom to plan for the honeymoon, but then you reminded me that I never do anything that's traditional, so I thought I'd plan what I wanted to do."

"Which is?"

Her hand slid a little higher on his thigh. Nick had let go of her foot and didn't make any further effort to restrain her movements.

"I'd like to stay in bed with you for the next forty-eight hours or so, maybe getting up from time to time to eat. I'd like to make love with you until I fall asleep, sleep with you in my arms, and wake up to make love with you again."

She paused, as though waiting for a response, but for the life of him Nick couldn't think of a thing to say. He just sat there and stared at her.

She continued, "After a few days we might rent a car and explore the area, maybe go to Disney World, or charter a boat. Whatever you think you'd like to do. I want to have the kind of honeymoon that we can describe to our children and grandchildren with relish. One that gets better and better with each retelling."

Somehow in the course of her conversation she managed to slide into his lap. She curled up against him, her head resting against his shoulder.

After a few moments he said, "I thought you moved out of the house."

"Well, actually I did. But I don't think there's going to be a problem getting my deposit or first month's rent back. I mean, I never did move in. In fact, most of my things are still packed in boxes. But I've decided to wait until we get home to worry about unpacking."

There was no way he could ignore the fact that Dani was in his lap and that both of them were nude. He wrapped his arms around her. God, she felt good. He'd missed her so much.

He took his time kissing her before he asked, "What changed your mind about leaving me?"

"I decided that without me in your life to liven it up a bit you would just get bored. I didn't want that to happen to you."

He grinned. "You do manage to keep me off balance, don't you?"

"Well," she replied modestly, "I've had a lot of practice, you see. All those years of training didn't go for nothing."

"Dani?"

"Hmmm?"

"I love you so much."

She sighed, hearing the underlying emotion that she had not been attuned to hear until she'd read what he'd written about his feelings. Words were so inadequate, sometimes, to truly express what a person was feeling. Now that she realized that, she knew what she needed to do to let him know that his love was returned.

"Nick, there will never be another man in my life. You have been all I ever wanted or needed. I don't want to give you up. I love you and want to share your life."

"Did you mean what you said about children?"

She grew quiet. "I can't imagine having children without you as their father. But I'm not sure that I'm ready for a family right away." She placed her cheek against his. "Of course I didn't think I was ready for a husband six months ago, and I managed to adjust to that idea fairly rapidly."

"But we agreed that it would be temporary."

"No, we didn't. We agreed to take it one day at a time and see how things worked out. Well, I for one think they worked out very nicely, except that you apologized for making love to me." She leaned back and looked at him. "Please don't apologize, okay?"

He closed his eyes in remembered pain. "But I felt like I was taking advantage of you."

She nodded. "If that night was your idea of taking advantage of me, then you have permission to take advantage of me as often as you like. In fact, I insist on it."

He kissed her once more, this time showing her beyond any doubt that he would have no trouble following her suggestion.

When they finally broke apart, Nick said, "If we don't get out of here soon, we're going to drown." He stepped out of the tub and quickly dried himself, then lifted her out and hastily ran a towel over her. Tossing the towel aside, he picked her up and strode into the bedroom.

"Should I ask where we're going, Nick?"

He glanced down at her. "Honey, if you have to ask my intentions after all these years, you don't know me nearly as well as I thought."

Dani had almost made the biggest mistake in her life by not understanding Nick and his feelings for her. She knew she'd never make that mistake again.

Epilogue

"Damn it, Dani. Why did you take so long to call me? You never think ahead, do you? I can't trust you to look after yourself for a moment. I swear, if you ever—"

"Nick."

"What!"

"I'm okay, really I am."

"I just don't understand why you stayed at work late when you knew you'd be there by yourself. Anything could have happened and no one would have known about it."

"But nothing happened."

"What do you mean, nothing happened!"

"All right, so maybe I shouldn't have planned to work this long. But the doctor assured me that everything was fine. How was I to know that I'd go into labor three weeks early?"

Nick tried to concentrate on his driving and not on the woman who sat so quietly beside him. She would be the death of him yet. If his heart didn't give out, his blood pressure would cause a stroke.

"Dani. The one thing that I know about you, the one thing I can absolutely count on, is the fact that you act before you think. Why should I expect you to do something so out of character as thinking ahead, weighing the possible consequences now, just because you're ready to give birth?"

"There's no reason to get upset, Nick. Really."

"I let you convince me that pregnant women work all the time and that it's no problem."

"And I've had no problems."

"But I never suspected you would leave yourself in such a vulnerable spot."

She sighed. "I know. I'm just glad the security guard was so quick to respond to my call." She smiled. "See? I wasn't really alone."

"What if you'd fallen?"

"I didn't fall. I just wasn't expecting my first contractions to be quite so insistent."

"How far apart are they now?"

"Who's counting? Close enough, I'm sure."

He reached for her hand. "We should never have decided to do this."

She rolled her eyes. "Now he tells me."

"You're too tiny."

"The doctor said the baby is also small."

"You said you weren't ready for children."

She stared at him in disgust. "That was five years ago while we were on our honeymoon, Nick! A lot can happen in five years."

"I suppose."

"We've taken several trips overseas, you've had your first novel published and another show on Broadway."

"You're head of the research-and-development department at Merrimac," he added.

She smiled. "Yes. I'm very pleased with that."

"But a baby is going to make a big difference in our lives."

"Nick, I don't know how to break the news to you, love. But this sort of conversation should take place before the possibility of a pregnancy occurs, not while you're rushing your extremely pregnant wife to the hospital for delivery."

"I know," he groaned.

She patted his hand. "Everything's going to be all right. You'll see."

As soon as they turned into the hospital driveway Nick got into the lane to go to the emergency entrance.

"Nick, this isn't an emergency. Let's go in the front way and check in. I'm preregistered. All we have to do is let them know I'm here."

"Did you remember to call the doctor?"

She grinned. If he didn't trust her to think ahead, why would he think she'd call her doctor? "I've spoken with her," she said in her most soothing voice. "Everything is going along according to schedule. She should be here by the time I get upstairs."

He found a parking place and pulled in. He was opening her door before she had finished releasing her safety belt. He scooped her up in his arms and strode to the front door.

"Put me down, Nick. I'm too heavy for you to carry."

He glanced down at her in astonishment. "Too heavy! You've got to be kidding. You still aren't as heavy as normal-size people."

Looking down at her protruding midsection, Dani didn't consider herself to be a normal-size person. But Nick was in no shape to discuss the matter.

Poor darling. She had never seen Nick so rattled in all the years she'd known him. No crisis, no danger had unhinged him, so she'd had no suspicion that something as normal as childbirth would cause him to lose his famous composure.

And yet she should have known. The way he'd taken the news that she was pregnant, for instance.

They'd been in Paris. She's awakened that morning disgustingly nauseous. He'd found her hovering over the commode in the bathroom. After dampening a washcloth and bathing her face with it, Nick had knelt beside her. "What's the matter, honey? Was the food too rich for you last night? Do you think you've picked up a bug or something?"

She'd muttered her first thought out loud. "I think I'm pregnant."

She struggled to her feet and looked at her white face in the mirror, then glanced down at Nick, who looked even whiter than she did.

"Pregnant?"

She turned and found her way back to the bed. Sinking thankfully back into the warm comfort of the covers, she merely nodded.

He followed her back into the bedroom and sank down beside her. "Are you sure?"

She rolled over and looked at him. He was definitely in shock. She felt a little sorry for him. "No, not absolutely positive. But all the signs are there, especially after that little round." She took his hand and cradled it against her cheek. "It isn't as though we've tried to prevent a pregnancy since we left home this time. I thought you wanted children."

"I do. I guess I just hadn't thought about how it would affect you."

"Don't worry about it. Maybe morning sickness won't linger," she said hopefully.

He gathered her into his arms. "Oh, Dani. I want to protect you from pain. Instead, I seem to be responsible for inflicting more on you."

Months later, Dani remembered his words and almost groaned. She knew that she wasn't going to be able to hide the intensity of her contractions from Nick much longer. The hospital personnel had wasted no time in getting her to bed. She wanted to send Nick away but knew better than to try. He'd insisted on taking the childbirth classes with her. She wasn't at all sure she could handle his reaction to her pain.

"Nick?"

"Yes, darling," he responded quickly, holding her hand.

"I was wondering if you would do me a favor?"

"Anything. Name it."

"Would you mind calling my mother and telling her we're here?"

"Now?" His tone held a hint of disbelief.

"They'll want to come."

"But I thought I could call afterwards."

"I really would rather know—" she had to wait to find the breath to continue "—that they were on their way."

Reluctantly he left her and she silently prayed he wouldn't find a phone right away, that he wouldn't find the change, that her parents would be slow to answer, that . . .

"Easy now, easy. You're doing just fine, Mrs. Montgomery, just fine," one of the nurses said.

"I don't want my husband to see me in pain," she panted after a few moments.

"Honey, there's no one here who'll be able to keep your husband away from you. So you might as well get used to the idea."

Dani lost track of what was happening around her. She was too busy concentrating on what her body was doing. She realized at one point that

Nick was there, quietly coaching her, his voice low and soothing.

Why had she worried about him? Nick was always there for her. He always had been. He always would be....

"Would you like to hold your daughter, Mr. Montgomery?" one of the nurses asked Nick some time later. They had cleaned the squirming red-faced mite, wrapped her in a pink blanket and held her out to him.

Nick took the bundle gingerly, still overwhelmed by the miracle he had just witnessed. Dani lay quietly, her eyes closed, as the doctor continued to work with her. Nick looked down at the tiny scrap of humanity in the blanket and felt such an outpouring of love that he could no longer contain the feelings, but he ignored the tears that slid down his cheeks.

She was tiny, his daughter. Like her mother. Short wisps of black hair curled around her head. She kept blinking her eyes as though even the muted light in the room was too bright for her. When at last she opened them he saw Dani staring at him once again. The love he felt continued to magnify.

"Is she all right?" Dani asked, her voice barely audible.

"She's perfect," Nick managed to reply. "Just like her mother." He placed the baby in Dani's arms. "It never occurred to me before that if I did everything right in this lifetime I would be blessed with two of you."

Dani gave him a sleepy smile. "You mean you haven't grown tired of being my guardian and protector? You want more of us around?"

He cleared his throat. "Always and forever. Don't ever forget it."

* * * * * *

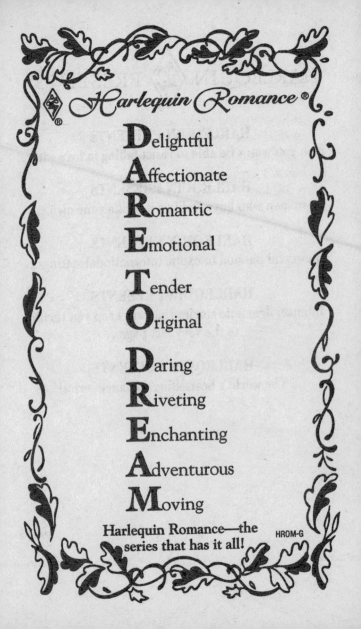

Harlequin Romance ®

Delightful

Affectionate

Romantic

Emotional

Tender

Original

Daring

Riveting

Enchanting

Adventurous

Moving

Harlequin Romance—the
series that has it all!

HROM-G

HARLEQUIN PRESENTS®

HARLEQUIN PRESENTS
men you won't be able to resist falling in love with...

HARLEQUIN PRESENTS
women who have feelings just like your own...

HARLEQUIN PRESENTS
powerful passion in exotic international settings...

HARLEQUIN PRESENTS
intense, dramatic stories that will keep you turning
to the very last page...

HARLEQUIN PRESENTS
The world's bestselling romance series!

SPECIAL EDITION

Stories of love and life, these powerful
novels are tales that you can identify with—
romances with "something special" added in!

Fall in love with the stories of authors such
as **Nora Roberts, Diana Palmer, Ginna Gray**
and many more of your special favorites—as
well as wonderful new voices!

Special Edition brings you
entertainment for the heart!

SSE-GEN

WAYS TO *UNEXPECTEDLY* MEET MR. RIGHT:

♡ Go out with the sexy-sounding stranger
your daughter secretly set you up with
through a personal ad.

♡ RSVP yes to a wedding invitation—soon
it might be your turn to say "I do!"

♡ Receive a marriage proposal by mail—
from a man you've never met....

These are just a few of the unexpected
ways that written communication
leads to love in Silhouette Yours Truly.

Each month, look for two fast-paced, fun and
flirtatious Yours Truly novels
(with entertaining treats and sneak previews
in the back pages) by some of your favorite
authors—and some who are sure to
become favorites.

YOURS TRULY™:
Love—when you least expect it!

Elizabeth Taylor
and
Eddie Fisher

When Elizabeth Taylor married Mike Todd, husband number three of eight, in 1957, Eddie Fisher was the best man and his then wife Debbie Reynolds was the matron of honor. After Todd's death in a plane crash a year later, Eddie and Debbie comforted a devastated Elizabeth. A relationship developed between Elizabeth and Eddie, and amid a scandal, the couple married in 1959. They divorced five years later, after Elizabeth met her fifth husband, actor Richard Burton, on the film set of *Cleopatra*.